BOOK THREE
OF THE AUN SERIES

DAUGHTER
OF
TWO
WORLDS

LEE BEZOTTE

INSPARKET
MEDIA

This book is dedicated to the quirky, misunderstood daughters and sons. Our world would be drab and dull without you.

CHAPTER ONE
Two Worlds

"THIS TIME YOU WON'T ESCAPE me, Smarmy Kidd Black!" Maren shouted as she playfully smacked her mule with a twig.

Don't bet on it! she imagined him to reply. *The rest of my pirate gang will be along any minute.*

"Well, if they come, they'll fall right into my trap," the young girl whooped as the cold wind whipped her long hair into slender, dark fingers that danced in the air. Though she preferred to wear an elegant woolen dress every day, her appearance was wild and unkempt, and she seldom cleaned up without significant coaxing. On this day, she was especially filthy since that was the state in which she envisioned her swashbuckling alter ego to be. Adding to her zealous warning she let out a forceful, "Ha ha ha ha haaaa!"

Interrupting her daydream, she heard the voice of Son call out, "Stop torturing Earl and come help in the garden!"

Maren stopped what she was doing as her fantasy threatened to evaporate in the breeze. She massaged her right ear and looked in her guardian's direction with a blank expression. As she stood there, she continued the scene she was acting out in a quiet whisper, not really paying attention to what was being spoken to her. In her mind, the story had begun and she could not give audience to anything else until its completion.

"This is the third time I've called you to come over," the boy chided. "We all have to do our chores or we won't be able to plant on time."

As he was still talking, Maren moved onto the donkey's back and grabbed a handful of his mane. "I'm just going to put Earl in the barn first," she explained.

"Okay, but please do hurry," Son said. "I'm going to have to go inside to start dinner soon."

Ignoring his urging, the girl rode slowly up toward the barn, continuing her fanciful adventure in a hushed voice. "Get moving, Smarmy Black. I'm taking you to prison."

No cell can hold me for long, the mule replied. *And when I get out, I'll have my revenge.* He then whinnied and shook his head as he plodded along past the garden.

When they reached the barn, Maren slid off of the donkey's back, opened the door, and led him inside. She then turned around and closed the door so that both of them were shut in together, allowing her to play, for a little while longer, outside of the view of others.

"What should we read, Earl?" she asked the animal as she ran to the back of the barn where several of her books were stashed.

You decide, she imagined him to say.

"All right then, I choose *The Marauders of Mydais*," she announced.

As she searched for the book, Earl sniffed at the floor,

lowered his head, and slowly brought himself down into a bed of hay and wood shavings. Once situated, he munched on the hay contentedly, occasionally looking up at her. Once she found the book she was looking for, she ran over to him, sat down, and leaned back against his side.

As she read aloud, her mind took her far away to fantastic adventures and perilous escapes. She had no idea how much time had passed until the waning light in the barn made it difficult to keep reading.

She was about to put the book away and head to the garden when she heard Son yell, "Maren! Dinner!"

Immediately, she returned the book to its place in the back of the barn and ran to the house to eat.

Son sat across the small kitchen table from Maren, watching the steam rise from his bowl and pondering the last few days. As they ate the vegetable soup he had prepared, he wished that Dulnear and Faymia would hurry home from their hunting trip. Whenever his patience with Maren would run low, Faymia always seemed to have the right thing to say, and an endless gracious tone.

Trying his best to sound gentle yet firm, he said to the girl, "Maren, I really need you to keep up with your chores. I can't run the farm all by myself."

Looking down into her bowl of soup, she said, "I know," and slurped up another spoonful.

"This is very important," her guardian added.

"I know," she said again, making an odd face at the carrots dancing about in their pool of warm broth.

Suspecting that she wasn't really listening, Son's neck

stiffened. His lips tightened and he spoke a little louder. "Look at me, Maren."

The girl massaged her ear and stared blankly up at the young man.

"Many times today, I called you over and tried to get you to help in the garden but you never came," he complained. "Why don't you just stop playing and come?" he asked.

Still staring, Maren answered plainly, "I came when you called for dinner."

Frustrated that she seemed to be missing the point he was trying to make, Son's face grew flush and his voice raised even more. "That's what I'm trying to explain," he said. "You don't want to do your part but you certainly want to eat your fill."

Just then, a strange half-smile began to curl upward from the left side of Maren's mouth. It was as if an unseen finger was pushing it, and a quiet chuckle forced its way out through her nose.

Offended that the girl seemed to find humor in his frustration, his cheeks burned and his blue eyes narrowed. "This isn't humorous!" he snapped. "Why are you laughing?"

Maren seemed genuinely surprised by Son's anger. She massaged her ear more aggressively, swallowed, and answered, "I was thinking about Smarmy Kidd Black."

Son glared at the young girl. He was beside himself with the feeling that she neither desired to do her part, nor cared how her distraction impacted his burden of responsibility. He wanted to accuse her of laughing at him. He wanted to scold her harshly and send her to bed. His inability to discern whether he was dealing with Maren's graymind or just rude behavior made choosing a response difficult.

Finally, he took a deep breath, exhaled, and admonished, "I'm glad that you like your books. Fantastic stories of pirates and adventure are exciting and fun. However, we live in a real world where chores need to be done, your clothes need to be washed, and your hair needs to be brushed. Ignoring the things you need to do now only brings more trouble and work later."

The girl continued to stare at Son with a vacant expression. Eventually, her eyes focused on his. As they did, she cleared her throat and said, "I like my stories. They're my friends."

The young caretaker tried hard to comprehend what the girl meant. He wished to impress upon her some sort of virtue that she would grasp, so he began, "You are part of the Great Father's story. It is the greatest tale ever written and you get to choose your role in it." He then paused to consider his words. "Will your role be that of a character who spends their days in a trance, shackled by entertainment and indulgence? Or will it be that of a hero, choosing the difficult yet rewarding challenges of life? Do you want to be a main character or a footnote? The choice is yours, Maren." Feeling satisfied with his speech, he then relaxed and lifted a spoonful of soup to his mouth.

Maren's eyes slowly turned downward to her soup. She stirred her spoon in the bowl, causing the vegetables to race around the sides of the bowl as they crashed into each other. She then finished her dinner without saying another word.

That evening, as Maren lay down in her bed, she gazed into the darkness of her modest bedroom. As she did, she spoke out loud, as if someone was there with her. "I'm an excellent gardener," she said. "In fact, I'm one of the best. But someone has to keep the farm safe from pirates. They're an ever-present danger!"

The girl couldn't understand why Son seemed so upset at dinner. It was unreasonable for him to be cross just because she didn't do her chores right away. After all, she said she would do them and her word was her bond. If he was impatient, then that was his problem. "Maybe if you spent more time patrolling, then I wouldn't have to," she continued to argue. "And who else is going to keep Earl company?" she added. "You know he's fragile."

As the night drifted on, Maren's thoughts shifted. It had been a couple of years since she had lost her parents on the road from Ahmcathare to Blackcloth, and she still missed them dearly. Though she struggled to recall specific experiences, she pined for her mother's calm voice and friendly flow. "What a wonderful drawing!" she said in her best grown-up voice.

"Why thank you, Momma," she answered back in her own. "I drew it for you."

"You are very special to me and Daddy," the grown-up voice added.

With that, a tear found its way out of the young girl's eye and was followed by a burning sensation. She wiped her cheek with the back of her hand and then touched her tongue to the tear so she could taste the saltiness. "Uh huh," she said back in her own voice.

Another tear came, and then another, until her tired eyes grew heavy and she succumbed to dreams and shadows.

The next morning, Maren sat reading a book on the back of her mule as it grazed about the farm. It was still early in the season and patches of tender grass weren't easy to find. As Earl roamed about, the young girl made sure to steer him away from places that Son could easily see as he was working in the garden.

"We can't be seen by Dirtclod McGee," she warned the donkey.

Why not? she imagined the mule asking before he gathered another mouthful of cold, damp grass.

"Because he will enslave us and force us to work in the potato mines," she explained.

Ah, the potato mines. I'll never go back there, Earl declared. *Your safety is my first charge, m'lady.*

"Then ride on," Maren ordered before returning to her book. As she read the tale aloud, she lost herself within a world of magic heroes and devious enemies, acting out each scene as if she were experiencing everything the main characters were experiencing. Though there was peril and adventure on every page, she somehow felt safe in that world. The wind was never too cold, the labor never too hard, and the people were as lovely and colorful as she imagined them to be. She never really feared the villains because they always lost in the end, and the brave champions had no flaws, never raised their voices, and never made the other characters do their chores. She often wished that she could live inside of her books, and it made her grumpy when she had to put them away.

As the morning grew late, Earl found grass growing

more plentifully where the ground sloped up to meet the road. He continued to chomp, then move on to the next patch of green, until the farm gradually faded in the distance behind them.

When Maren looked up from her book, she realized that they were headed toward the village, away from the house. Her first feelings were of panic and dread, but those quickly turned to relief. "We did it!" she declared. "We escaped from Dirtclod McGee! He won't be bothering us now!"

Let's hope we can avoid his accomplices, the mule returned.

"Yes, we have to keep going," she said, and they traveled all the way into Laor.

Laor was a small town with a pub, an inn, and a few shops situated around a square. As they were approaching the village, Maren noticed that there were many more people milling about than usual. They were enjoying pastries, laughing, and carrying on about a festival. Moving closer to the square, she could hear music and see folks dancing and celebrating. The smells and sounds of fun and merriment roused her senses. It had been a long time since she had seen such a sight.

Maren's heart beat faster and an excitement rose up in her chest. She couldn't believe her luck. She tied her mule to a nearby hitching post and began walking around the outside of the crowd, searching for the source of those delicious-looking pastries. Finally, she approached a boy who appeared to be about her age. He dressed differently from the children she usually saw in Laor. His clothing looked expensive, and he had dark-brown hair that swept across his forehead. Before she had a chance to say anything to him, he introduced himself. "I'm Micah, what's your name?" he asked.

"Maren," she replied eagerly. "How can I partake in the celebration?"

"Oh, I'll show you," Micah offered happily. "It doesn't even cost anything."

"Really?" the girl asked. "What do I have to do?"

"Just come to the inn with me," he said. "You just have to write your name down and you can have all the food you want. You can watch a show or go dancing too!"

"That sounds wonderful!" Maren declared. She paused for a moment and surveyed the scene once more. As she did, she noticed the boy hold out his hand and urge her once more to join him. She didn't take it, but she followed him into the crowd and across the square to the inn.

CHAPTER TWO

Indulgences

FAYMIA CROUCHED ON ONE KNEE behind a cluster of blackthorn shrubs. With bow drawn and her powerful silver eye fixed on a wise elk grazing in the near distance, she waited motionless for the majestic animal to expose its side. He's toying with me, she thought to herself. I don't know how much longer I can hold my arrow back. Her shoulder burned and her fingers were cold as she steadily held her position.

Just as her arm began to shake, a clicking sound emanated from a lone crow perched in a nearby tree. The beast turned its head toward the noise, exposing its neck for a brief moment, but that was all the skillful hunter needed. She released her bow and, in an instant, the arrow was buried deep into the elk's neck.

The animal darted away from the blackthorns with surprising speed. As Faymia pulled back another arrow, she heard a deep whoosh above her head as Dulnear leapt clear over her—and the shrubs—in a single bound. He landed on both feet and immediately gave chase. With his large form between the woman and the animal she was unable to land another arrow, so she tore after her husband, and the beast, into the woods.

Many lengths behind, Faymia could barely see the massive antlers of the wise elk bouncing and weaving, occasionally being pulled back when the arrow protruding from its neck would catch a tree as it sped by. Behind it was a blur of fur and steel as Dulnear pursued with a large hunting knife attached to his right arm where his hand should have been.

As the chase continued, the woman noticed that the ground began to slope downward and her strides were getting longer. Her heart raced as trees sped by at increasing speed and greater difficulty of dodging. Something suddenly occurred to her. "It's headed for the cliff!" she shouted out to the man from the north. "Just let it go!"

As she did her best to slow her speed, her stomach turned over as she saw the elk's antlers, and then the warrior, suddenly disappear beneath the horizon. "Dulnear!" she cried out in panic.

Faymia quickly but carefully approached the cliff's edge. As she peered downward, she was awash with relief to see her husband standing on a narrow ledge just a few feet below. He had cut the elk from where the arrow had been lodged in its neck, down to its collar bone. Its life had been spilled out into the sea below. "This knife-hand that Son made me is amazing!" he yelled up to her with an enthusiastic smile.

With equal parts fondness and frustration, the hunter shouted down, "You didn't need to chase him. One more arrow and he would have laid down for us."

"That does not sound very fun," the man replied.

"Neither does hauling that elk up here and back to the horses," she said through pursed lips.

The smile faded from the warrior's face as he exhaled and looked down at the slain animal. "You know that I love you, Faymia."

"Of course," she said as the corners of her mouth crept wryly upward.

"Will you please bring the horses here?" he asked with a sheepish expression growing across his face.

The sweet sound of the woman's laughter filled the air and she turned away. "I'll be right back," she announced. "Try not to kill anything else while I'm gone."

○

"What's yer name and where do you live, sweetie?" the smiling old man asked. He was seated behind a cluttered table just in front of the inn.

There was something about the man that made Maren nervous. He had long, dirty, gray hair and he reeked of smoke. Her enthusiasm waned considerably, and she turned back to look at Micah.

"It's okay," the boy assured her. "They just want to know who you are so they can invite you back to celebrations in the future."

This explanation comforted the girl somewhat, and she spoke up, "Maren. I live at Gale Hill Farm."

"Very good!" the man behind the table said as he scribbled the information on a parchment. "You've come on a good day. There are pastries and cakes across the square and outside of the pub, and fresh roasted meat next to that. Also, there's lots of music and dancing all day." He then stood up, reached across the table, and tied a small red ribbon around her wrist, saying, "You'll need to keep this on."

Maren liked the way the ribbon looked. She smiled and then did a little jig to show her fondness for dancing.

"Wonderful!" the man applauded, clapping his hands. "I'm sure the two of you will have a splendid time."

"Uh huh!" the girl agreed, and met eyes with her new friend once more. "I think I'll start with some sweets."

"Great idea!" Micah cheered. "Let's go. They have a delicious cream pie." He then began to skip in that direction with Maren in tow.

When they arrived outside of the pub, there were several people crowded around tables filled with the most gorgeous desserts the girl had ever seen. She approached one of them and eyed a fresh blackberry pie. Standing behind the table was a plump, drained-looking woman who smiled wanly at her and asked, "What can I get you, darlin'?"

Maren smiled and pointed at the pie she wanted. Her mouth watered and she swallowed in anticipation.

"Right then," the woman said as she set a generous slice onto a tin plate, heaped fresh whipped cream on top, and handed it to her with a spoon that looked big enough to feed a large man.

The girl nodded in gratitude and turned around toward Micah. "There are tables over there," the boy told her, pointing to an area at the edge of the town square. He then began walking in that direction.

Maren followed him, half watching the ground and half watching to make sure nothing slid off of her plate. The tables were full of festivalgoers but the boy found one with two empty seats across from each other.

From where she sat, the girl could see most of the goings on in the village. She watched as folks ate, laughed, and mingled, and was once again astounded by her good fortune to have wandered into town on such a day as this. She then took her spoon and scooped as much pie and whipped cream onto it as would fit and stuffed a surprising amount of it into her mouth.

The pie had an unexpected taste on her tongue. Though it seemed to promise to be the best dessert she had ever eaten, it was average at best. It was not bad, but not exquisite either. At first, she was disappointed, but she continued to eat it anyway.

"How's the pie?" Micah asked her with an amused expression.

"Okay," she answered before devouring more whipped cream and blackberries.

"I've eaten loads of sweets today," the boy proclaimed as he puffed out his chest. "No one can eat more than me!"

Maren laughed through a mouth full of dark-purple berries, then forced another bite.

"What sort of things do you like to do?" Micah asked as his eyes followed her spoon.

The girl's eyes lit up with his question. She grinned with pie-smudged teeth and answered, "Draw pictures, play with my mule, and read pirate stories."

"Pirate stories. You don't say!" the boy replied. "What's so special about pirates?"

Maren's excitement grew as she began talking about pirate adventures with an interested listener. "I read all the books, and I pretend my mule is Smarmy Kidd Black. He's the most treacherous pirate on the nine seas! His ship has a crew of a hundred and fifty men and thirty trained dogs! Each of those dogs is named Typhoon, and their tails have been cut off so that they don't smack anyone when they're wagging them. Also, the ship has never been boarded by a child or a woman. Did you know that?"

Micah's eyebrows raised as the young girl carried on with enormous amounts of information about life on the sea, swashbuckling, and the various minutia of ship rigging. When she finally stopped talking for a moment, he complimented, "You sure know a lot about pirates."

"Uh huh!" she agreed. She then continued on with the names of all one hundred and fifty crew members, and how they are able to call the dogs to them, even though they are all named Typhoon. It was a long, drawn-out presentation, but it was worth it to educate her new friend on the ways of buccaneering in the world of her favorite books.

"Well," the boy eventually broke in. "Um, did you know that there will be a book reading near the inn in just a wee bit?"

"I read books all the time," she answered plainly, surprised that he hadn't already picked up on that.

"No, I mean that someone will be reading a book out loud to everyone," he said.

Maren's cheeks raised at the thought of hearing a story told to the festivalgoers. Reading to herself was nice, but there was something special about being read aloud to. Her mother used to spend endless hours reading to her when she was younger, but that was a very long time ago. "Let's go then!" she crowed. She then stuffed the remainder of the pie in her mouth and stood up to walk across the square.

As the afternoon progressed, it was more fun than the girl could have imagined. The stories were riotous and exciting, the food was rich and plentiful, and she had a friend who seemed interested in all she had to say about her favorite books and characters.

As the townspeople were making their way out of the square for the night, it dawned on Maren that she too had to make her way home. Lanterns around the town were being lit, and the shop windows were filling with the warm glow of fire from inside.

"Leaving?" asked Micah, still accompanying her through the thinning crowd.

Nervously massaging her ear, the girl replied, "Uh huh. I have to go to bed."

"There will be more festivities tomorrow," the boy informed her. "Will you be coming back?"

With that news, some of the nervousness dissipated from the girl's shoulders. "Okay," she replied with a half-smile.

But Maren didn't feel so well as she walked away from Micah and untied Earl from the post. Her belly was too full of sweets and rich foods and her head had a dull ache from the sights and sounds that overfilled her senses all day long. Despite how she felt, she still planned on returning the next day.

She walked her mule away from the village and toward the road leading home. As she did, the firelight that burned in the square faded into the distance and her surroundings became engulfed in a deep, black night. She wrung her hands as she stood in the road, mostly sure that she was facing the right direction. She hefted herself onto Earl's back, gave him a little squeeze with her legs, and instructed him to move along.

The animal ambled slowly, stopping often to sniff the ground along the way. Maren's slight uncertainty that they were traveling in the right direction, and the occasional sounds of animals in the distance, made her feel vulnerable and afraid.

"Why did you bring me out here?" she asked Earl in an accusatory tone.

You didn't have to stay as late as you did, she imagined him answering, matching her mood.

"They kept giving me pie," she said in her defense. "And the celebration just wouldn't end!"

Earl let out a *hrmph* before moving on to the next patch of ground that interested him.

Somewhere in the darkness behind her, two raccoons erupted into a violent skirmish. The sound startled Maren and she leaned forward, wrapping her arms around Earl's neck the best she could. She then rapidly tapped his sides with her heels, saying quietly, "Move on. Move on. Move on."

The beast walked forward more quickly, and she listened to make sure that the sound of the raccoons grew faint in the distance.

As the night grew later, the young girl's heart beat in her chest with crushing anxiety. The black was so great that she couldn't even see her mule. It was only the steadiness of his steps and the sound of his hooves against the pressed-down earth beneath them that assured her they were still on the road. "Get us home. Get us home," she whispered to him.

Just when tears were beginning to form in her eyes, Maren saw a light in the distance. As Earl took them closer, she recognized the window that it shone from. They were approaching the farm. "Maren!" she could hear Son yelling from the doorway of their home.

As her guardian's voice rang out, her anxiety turned to dread. She knew that he would not be happy with her for sneaking off, and she hated being scolded more than anything. So much so that she decided to travel down the road just a little further so she could make her way around to the barn without being seen. She got down from her donkey, used one hand to hold his rope, and groped through the darkness with the other hand until she had made her way around to the front of the building.

The girl quietly opened the barn door and led Earl inside. Wanting desperately to remain unnoticed, she felt her way to the back and found a pile of hay to lie down on. Lying there, her tummy uncomfortably full and her neck itching from the hay, she listened to Son continue to call out her name. Each time he did, she wished he would be quiet so she could go to sleep.

She had spent the day feasting on only the foods she enjoyed. She was entertained for endless hours. She danced, talked about things that interested her, and made a new friend. Even though the journey home was dark and frightening, she could only think about one thing, and that was going back to the festivities the next day.

CHAPTER THREE

Nothing is Free

"MAREN! WHAT ARE YOU DOING out here?" Son asked in a loud, clear tone.

The young girl sat up in the pile of hay and wood shavings and tried to blink away the sleep from her eyes. Her fingers were stained with blackberries and she used them to massage her right ear. She knew she had done the wrong thing by sneaking off and she heard a ringing in her head as her surroundings began to spin. She swallowed hard and answered quietly, "Um, I went into town."

"What?" the boy asked with wrinkles quickly forming on his forehead.

"Earl took me into Laor," she answered, sitting up a little taller.

"What do you mean by that?" Son asked. His neck pulled back as if to join his forehead in concern.

"I was riding Earl, and he wandered down the road," she explained.

"Why didn't you stop him and lead him back?"

"I don't know," she answered. "I was just reading a book,

and that idiot mule took me all the way to Laor." She hoped that by placing the attention on poor Earl, it would move the boy's focus off of her.

He exhaled, clearly exasperated by her story. "If you would have been doing your long-overdue chores, you wouldn't have ended up in the village."

Maren continued to squeeze her ear. It helped to ease her nerves. She stared off in the direction of Son without meeting his eyes with hers. As she did, she remained speechless.

Squinting, the boy asked, "What's on your fingers, and around your lips?"

"Um, blackberries," she answered, swallowing again.

"Blackberries?"

"From blackberry pie."

"Where did you get blackberry pie?"

"In town," she answered, wondering how Son could miss such an obvious deduction.

"But *how* did you get it?" the boy pressed. "You don't have any money."

"My friend Micah," she answered with deliberate vagueness.

Son raised one eyebrow and cocked his head to the side. "Friend Micah? How do you know him?"

"I met him yesterday," she answered, still wondering how Son could miss such conspicuous details.

"How old is Micah?" he continued to probe, obviously not ready to let the matter go.

Maren stood up, brushed the hay from her dress, and held her hand level just above her head. "He's about this tall," she explained. "He invited me to come back today for sweets and music."

The boy furrowed his brow and took a deep breath. "Well, I don't want you to go anywhere until your chores are done," he said. "Get caught up the best you can, then you can clean up and go. And you must be home before dark," he added. "No exceptions."

Maren's eyes betrayed that she was hiding a smile. She quickly grabbed Earl's rope and made her way past Son, rushing toward the barn door. Before she could leave, her guardian gently put his hand on her shoulder and said, "I was very worried about you last night."

Glancing back toward him, the girl said simply, "I know." She then skipped out to the garden to catch up on her work.

○

As Son stood at his workbench in the barn, he was deep in thought about Maren's story. When he'd discovered her alone on the road to Blackcloth more than two seasons ago, he knew it was the right thing to take her in and care for her. However, he himself hadn't even reached adulthood yet, and he struggled daily to be patient with her. Even more so when it came to her graymind.

It's like I am speaking a language she doesn't understand, he thought to himself. *And she is speaking a language I don't understand. I only wish there was a way...*

As his thoughts trailed off, he worked diligently at his bench to make toys to sell in Laor. He often brought his creations into the village to earn extra money. His favorite was the miniature trebuchet. He loved to see the looks on the children's faces when he demonstrated it for them. Their eyes would light up when the device's arm would swing around, flinging a pebble into the distance. They would laugh and run to their parents to beg them to purchase one for them. He sold more of the little hurlers than anything else.

He toiled the morning away shaping branches, twine, and stones. It was an activity he could easily lose himself in. When he came to a place in his work that required him to stop and search the barn for more materials, he came across Maren's stash of adventure books. He picked one up and examined it. As he did, a nagging thought weighed on his mind.

Son had been going in to the village regularly ever since they moved onto Gale Hill Farm. He had sold many of his trinkets and gadgets and, in the process, had gotten to know the children in the area quite well. As their faces flashed through his mind, it occurred to him that he had never met a boy named Micah.

This troubled him, so he decided to go outside to ask Maren a few more questions. "Maren," he called out, but there was no answer. "Maren!" he called out again. He walked out to the garden and noticed a large pile of rocks that the girl had pulled from the soil. There were also some seeds scattered about haphazardly. She had done her chores and rushed back into town with Earl.

When Maren and her donkey arrived at the village, the square was already full of revelers and partygoers. She looked around for Micah but couldn't find him so she tied up Earl and made her way over to the sweets tables outside of the pub. Once again they were filled with decadent desserts of every kind. She slowly walked past the puddings and cakes and found that there was a fresh blackberry pie in the same place she had found one the day before.

She looked at the busy woman arranging the sweets and asked sheepishly as she licked her lips, "Excuse me. May I have a slice of pie, please?"

There was no answer from the harried worker, who continued to shift the desserts around and serve them up to other people.

Maren cleared her throat and spoke a little louder, "Excuse me. I need a slice of pie."

The woman glanced over at her and smiled. "Oh hello. I didn't see you there. What would you like?"

"Some pie, please," the little girl said curtly, and her eyes grew bigger.

"Okay, can I see your ribbon please?" the helper asked.

Believing the woman was wishing to admire the thin strip of red cloth, Maren held out her wrist with a proud smile.

"That's a red ribbon," the helper said plainly. "Today you have to have a blue ribbon."

The girl's face fell, and she was confused about what the woman had just told her. Then she remembered how she saw the man in front of the inn and that he gave her the red ribbon when she gave him her name and where she lived. She could see the man at his table from across the square so she walked over to him with a quickness, though she didn't want to appear to be running.

"May I have a blue ribbon please?" she asked as she approached the man. He was poring over a stack of papers and apparently didn't hear her. A moment later she asked again, "Do you have any blue ribbon?"

The man looked up and greeted, "Oh hiya, darlin'. What can I do fer ya?"

"I would like a blue ribbon," she said as she held out her red-ribboned wrist.

"Oh, I see," the man said. He shifted the papers aside and fetched a small spool of thinly cut fabric. Cutting just enough to tie around the girl's wrist, he announced, "That'll be two coppers, sweetie."

Maren froze. She had no money with her and none at home that she knew of. Her shoulders sank and she massaged her ear. "I don't have any coppers," she said.

"I'm sorry, honey. It's two coppers to be a part of the festivities today," the man explained.

The young girl glanced back toward the desserts, and all the people dancing and laughing. She felt pulled toward the food and revelry. Thinking fast, she asked, "Will you be here tomorrow?"

"Yes, ma'am," he said.

"Can I pay you tomorrow?"

The man wrinkled his forehead. "I have to take something today. Is there anything you can give me now?"

Maren thought for a moment as she fixed her eyes on the papers strewn across the table. Then she had an idea. "I can draw you a picture," she declared. She loved to draw and was very good at it.

The man rubbed his chin and pushed his whiskery lips to the side. "Hmmm. I'll have to ask Sevuss if that's okay. Stay put," he said. He then disappeared through the door behind him and into the inn.

Moments later, the man returned with an expensively dressed gent with wiry, ginger-and-white hair. His skin looked thin and leathery, and his teeth were tobacco-stained and crooked. Maren didn't like the look of the man, but she remained polite and composed anyway. "So, you don't have any money at all?" Sevuss asked with a perturbed expression smeared across his face.

"No," said the girl. "But I can draw you a picture."

"Pictures don't pay for all of this," the man in charge said as he gestured toward the festivities happening in the square. He then squinted and looked into the distance for a bit. Scratching his cheek, he offered, "I'll tell you what. Today I'll let you draw me a picture, but tomorrow you'll have to bring some money, or something more valuable than a few charcoal scratches on paper." He then nodded to the gray man behind the table and disappeared back into the inn.

"Yessir," Maren replied, even though Sevuss was already out of earshot.

"Well then," the man behind the table said as he handed Maren a few sheets of paper and a pencil. "It's your lucky day. You can stand at the edge of the table to make your drawings and bring them to me when they're ready."

"Okay," the girl said as she took the paper and found a clear spot to draw on.

She spent several minutes sketching a recreation of the town square with all of its party-goers, musicians, and spectators. It was difficult for her to be patient with the process because she was eager to join in the celebrating. When she was satisfied with the drawing, she walked over and handed it to the man.

"Well, that was quick," he said, sweeping his long, gray hair out of his eyes. He studied the image, looking up at the subject of the drawing and then back toward the paper. "This is very impressive," he said with an amused smile.

"I know," Maren replied. Her mouth was already watering for more blackberry pie.

The man looked over to the edge of the table, then back to the square, then at the drawing again. "You weren't even lookin' at the square. How'd ye draw it so well?"

"I remembered," she answered confidently.

"I'll say ye did," he said as he took a final peek at the sketch. He then picked up the blue ribbon he had cut for Maren earlier. "Well, let's tie this around yer arm. Would you like me to cut off the one from yesterday?"

"No, thank you," she said, and she held out her wrist, ready for an endless number of sweets and amusements. Once the fabric was secured, she ran off gleefully to take it all in.

CHAPTER FOUR

A Dearer Price

"THE ROAD IS UP AHEAD," Dulnear mentioned to Faymia. The elk they had hunted was stretched across a makeshift cart that was tied to both of their horses.

"It's about time," his wife responded. "I think we'll hunt closer to home next time. Dragging this carcass hasn't been easy."

The man from the north smiled. He had thoroughly enjoyed every part of their excursion together, even the challenge of hauling the game back home. "It has been wonderful to toil alongside of you, my love."

Faymia chuckled and her expression lightened. "Then perhaps we can toil a little harder together and finish building our cottage when we get back."

The large man's smile turned into a laugh. He had been working on a dwelling for the two of them for quite some time. It sat on the southern edge of Gale Hill Farm with a view of the distant sea on one side and kept Son and Maren's house within sight on the other. "It will make a fine place to grow old together," he said.

"Well, let's make sure we don't grow old before we can move in," she joked.

Around midday, the two hunters came upon a small village that was situated on either side of the easterly road. It was unique in that the northern half was partly built into a rocky hill, and the southern half was built on stilts to keep it level with the road. It was unusually quiet for the hour, and the street was littered with discarded papers, eating utensils, and the bones of various fowl.

Dulnear halted their horses and smelled the air as he looked around. The hair on the back of his neck felt like needles of ice. "This is not right," he said to Faymia in a hushed tone.

"It was a lovely town just a few days ago," she said.

They rode their horses up to the nearby tavern and tied them to a post. As they stepped inside, the man from the north noticed how few people were there for an afternoon meal. He also observed that those who were there were relatively quiet and bore somber expressions. Continually scanning the room, he approached the old barkeep, who was busy wiping down a clean countertop. "Good afternoon," he said, announcing his presence.

The barkeep looked up and seemed surprised by the presence of the considerable fur-clad warrior. "Good after-noon," he swallowed.

"Two mugs of ale, please," Dulnear ordered as Faymia joined him at the bar.

"Yessir," the barkeep replied and turned around momen-tarily to fetch the brew. Setting the full tankards on the counter, the man smiled awkwardly and exclaimed, "It's nice to get some business from the likes of folks like you today."

"What do you mean by that?" the man from the north asked.

"Well, I mean that there ain't hardly been any business since everyone went off," the old man explained as he toweled out a mug.

Dulnear furrowed his brow and examined the room once again. "Please continue explaining," he said.

"It's just that most of the town took off in wagons with a bunch of fancy-dressed gents the other day," the barkeep said with a tinge of annoyance in his voice.

As the man was describing the exodus of the townspeople, Faymia drew closer to Dulnear and clung tightly to his arm. He looked down at his wife, then back at the old man. "And what of the slovenly appearance of your village?"

"Oh, that would be the celebrations that went on for days before they up and left," the man said.

Dulnear knew exactly where the barkeep was going with his story, but he pressed anyway. "What kind of celebrations?"

"Grand ones! They started out free, too. Then, every day, they grew more grandiose, and the fancy-dressed fellas charged more and more for them. I don't know how they did it, but they got the people to keep coming back, and keep paying more and more until—"

"Until they agreed to go as slaves," the man from the north said, finishing the barkeep's sentence. He could feel Faymia trembling as she held onto him. Suddenly, his heart beat faster and he asked, "Which way were they headed?"

"East, toward Laor," the old man answered.

Dulnear could feel his wife's grip tighten like a vice

around his arm and his chest burned. "Where did you say?" he demanded.

"Laor," the barkeep confirmed.

The burning sensation in the warrior's chest spread upward to his face in blotches of red and pink. He struggled momentarily to focus his eyes on the man behind the bar. He inhaled deeply through flared nostrils and regained his focus. "Here is payment for the ale," he said as he dropped a couple of coins on the countertop. "We must be going."

"All right, Godspeed," the old man said, scratching the back of his head as he fixed his eyes on the northerner's troubled grimace.

Dulnear began to turn around with Faymia still holding firm to his arm. He then halted abruptly, remembering something. He glanced back at the barkeep and announced, "Thank you for the information. I will leave a freshly slain elk by your door."

The man wrinkled his forehead and squinted his eyes. "An elk? I don't need an elk."

"It is yours," the man from the north continued as he walked toward the exit.

"What am I going to do with—"

"Good day."

As Faymia and Dulnear rode east toward Laor, ill-tempered skies forced out cold rain, filling the narrow, winding road along the jagged hillside. It was slippery and dangerous but there was no stopping. Faymia's stomach turned at the idea of slavers in Laor. She herself had fallen into slavery for many years and was fortunate to have had help to get out.

Her imagination tormented her with thoughts of Son and Maren falling for the trap that is so skillfully set to ensnare people all over Aun. She drove her horse hard, not wanting to waste a single moment.

"Take it easy," the man from the north admonished as he struggled to keep up with her. "'Tis best to arrive a day late than not at all."

"But we may already be too late," Faymia contended. "Why did we choose to hunt so far away?!"

"Son is a wise lad and a warrior in his own right," Dulnear argued. "He would not easily fall into a slaver's snare."

"Perhaps, but what about Maren? I'm far more concerned about her ability to discern a ruse than I am with Son's," the woman explained. As she spoke, she risked a little more speed from Tapp as they passed rock, hill, and evergreen with panicked quickness.

Dulnear conceded, "Yes, she would be particularly susceptible to the slaver's type of deception. However, let us be careful."

As if in response to the northerner's warning, the next curve in the road revealed that the deluge of rain had washed away a large section of their path. Faymia's horse skidded to a stop at the edge of the temporary river that blocked their way. As she observed the obstacle before her, she clenched her teeth and cursed under her breath. "I can't believe this is happening!" she grumbled.

The man from the north stopped his horse and dismounted. He walked over to the flowing water and put his hand in. "Perhaps we can walk the horses through it," he said. He then jogged over to a nearby tree that had long ago died and he broke off a long, narrow branch.

"What are you going to do with that?" the woman asked.

"I need to see how deep it is," he explained, and he began to insert the branch into the flow.

Just then, the rushing water turned a cloudy brown and it filled with debris. A sound like thunder mixed with falling trees filled the air from above. "Look out!" Faymia cried, backing up her horse frantically.

The temporary river had transformed into a mudslide, bringing rocks and tall trees down like they were pebbles and grass. It was as if the road at that place had simply grown tired of clinging to the mountain and had fallen into the valley. Dulnear ran back in the direction they had come from as fast as he could, barely clearing the rush of destruction. His horse wasn't as fortunate and was swept away by the torrent. "Mor!!" he shouted as he watched her flail to keep her head above the rapidly descending slide.

Faymia's heart sank and time seemed to stand still, as it appeared they would not make it back to the farm when she had hoped. If only they would have ridden a little faster. If only it hadn't been raining so hard. She got down from her horse and joined her husband in the road. Standing in the rain together, she consoled, "I'm sorry about Mor. She was a loyal companion."

Dulnear closed his eyes in thought for a moment. He then opened them and said, "She will be missed. But we must get to higher ground so we can get around this rubbish and return to the children."

"How do you propose we do that?" she asked.

"Unfortunately, we will have to leave Tapp here. Carry what you can, and we will climb around."

The woman loved her horse and hated the idea of leaving

him behind. "I can't just leave him here!" she protested. But she knew in her heart that they would never make it to the other side of the mudslide with the animal.

"He is a bright horse," Dulnear assured her. "It would be a risk to his safety to make him climb up the hill. He will most likely find a way home on his own."

Faymia took her bow and a few other items from one of the saddlebags. She then walked around the horse, reached into the other saddlebag, and withdrew an iron object with leather straps attached to it. It resembled a fist and the top part of a man's forearm. "You may be needing this," she announced.

"Ah, thank you, my love," the man from the north said. "I am afraid my knife-hand went down the hillside with Mor."

"What would you do without me?" the woman teased (though she was quite serious).

"I shudder to think," he replied.

She then walked around to the front of the horse, gently stroked his head and told him, "Goodbye, my friend. Find your way home and I'll have a whole basket of apples waiting for you."

Tapp nodded his head as if he fully understood what she was saying.

Faymia took a deep breath and noticed that the rain had diminished to a sprinkle and the clouds had lightened into a pale gray. Much of the sliding earth and forest had slowed its descent into the valley, but it was still too dangerous to try to cross over. She looked up the damaged slope and declared, "I'm ready. Let's get to Laor."

"Okay," Dulnear answered. "Stay close."

○

As Son opened the door to look outside the barn, he could see Maren wrapping up her morning chores. The previous day's rain caused an abundant crop of weeds to spring up and he had checked on her work several times to make sure she didn't leave before the job was done.

For the last few days, he had been working hard to create several of his toys and gadgets to sell in Laor. He gathered from bits and pieces of conversation with the young girl that there was some sort of festival there and he reckoned it would be a great opportunity to make some silver.

"I'm done!" she shouted, and tossed a handful of earth and grass onto a pile before making her way to the barn to fetch Earl. She patted his saddlebag gently, grabbed his rope and made her way to the door.

"Okay," Son said. "But don't forget to be home before dark."

"I won't," she assured with a touch of annoyance in her voice. As she walked away with her mule, her young guardian noticed something.

"Maren," he said loudly to get her attention.

"What?" she replied curtly.

Son jogged so he could get in front of her and look at her from another angle. "You look different," he observed.

Maren's forehead wrinkled and she pushed her mouth to one side in a curious frown. As she massaged her ear with her free hand, she asked, "How do you mean?"

The boy squinted and cocked his head to the side. "You seem…heavier," he explained.

"Heavier?"

"Yes. But not taller."

"My dress is just getting smaller," she said.

The girl's assessment of the situation amused Son. He smiled and said, "I'm afraid it doesn't work that way. You must be eating too much when you're in the village. Do take care of yourself. Eating too many sweets isn't good for you."

Maren stared through the boy blankly as she continued to pull at her ear. Eventually, her eyes focused on his. "Um, okay," she said. "I'm going to go to Laor now."

Feeling leery, and not quite ready to see her leave, Son asked, "Will you be seeing your friend Micah?"

Maren's face became a little brighter and she answered, "Uh huh. He's there every day."

Son was happy that Maren had a friend. On many occasions he had invited her to join him when he went to sell his toys. He did so with the hope that she would make friends with other children in town. She mostly said no because she preferred to stay home. The times she did join him, she kept to herself or failed to find interest in what the other children were doing.

There was something nagging him about the boy Micah though. He tried to dismiss it as worry because he didn't know the name, but it kept coming back. "What does he look like?" he asked.

"He has nice clothes," she answered as she started to take the smallest of steps toward the road.

Son noticed her growing impatience and stepped to the side. Trying to catch her eyes, he said, "Well, please be careful. I haven't met the lad yet and I wouldn't want you to fall into bad company."

"I will," she assured with her eyes fixed on the road.

As Son watched her walk off, he felt a saddening sense of separation between himself and his young ward. He cared for her deeply, and would risk his life to protect her, but she seemed to be no more attached to him than she would be with a stranger. He wondered what their lives would become in the future, and carried his sadness with him for the rest of the day.

As Maren rode Earl into Laor, she noticed straightaway that there was a large tent erected in the town square. She could hear music and laughter and saw people coming and going with drinks and plates of food. She hopped off of Earl, quickly tied him to a post, grabbed the contents of his saddlebag, and ran over to the table situated in front of the inn.

"Well hello, Maren," the man with long, gray hair greeted her.

"Hello," Maren returned as she held out her arm so the man could cut yesterday's ribbon off. "Why is there a tent?" she asked.

"Well, today we have a special show," he answered. "We have a magician performing incredible feats. It's a marvel!"

"It's a marvel!" the girl repeated quietly as laughter hid just beneath her words.

"What do you have for me today?" the man asked as he grabbed a pair of scissors and a roll of green ribbon.

"This," she said as she set one of Son's contraptions on the table.

The worn-looking man frowned. "Now, Maren, you've already brought enough of those toys. I told you that yesterday."

"But I've already given up all my coins, my other dress, and my hairbrush," she protested.

The man folded his arms and rubbed his whiskery chin. Squinting, he asked, "How about that mule over there? He should do fine as payment."

The enthusiasm drained from Maren's shoulders and a thick heaviness overtook her ability to move. She swallowed, and the man standing behind the table looked to be growing larger and smaller at the same time. Her thoughts, however, blazed through her mind like a raging whirlwind of pros, cons, debate, and rationalization.

That old mule is constantly getting me into trouble, she thought to herself. She needed to think it because she loved Earl and didn't want to let him go. The pie that seemed only passable a few days ago was now the tastiest thing she'd ever put in her mouth, and she wanted more.

He's so stubborn, and he never goes where I want him to go, she continued. The words in her head came easier now as she compared having the troublesome donkey to what she was going to get to enjoy inside of the tent. *It would be best to let him go.*

Suddenly, a familiar voice from behind interrupted her thinking. "Whatcha doin'?" Micah asked.

Maren looked back to see him holding a plate full of sweets. "He wants my mule," she explained.

"That old thing? You're better off without him," he said as he stepped forward to stand beside her at the table.

Maren took her left ear and began massaging it. Now that her friend had confirmed that she should get rid of the animal, it made it easier to make her decision. She cleared her throat, held out her arm, and declared with a forced smile, "You can have him."

"That's a girl," the man behind the table said as he tied the green ribbon around her wrist. "Now you go and have a wonderful time. I'll take care of the mule."

"I will," she replied, and she spent the day marveling at the magician, filling up her belly, and forgetting about her faithful mule, Earl.

CHAPTER FIVE

A Business Transaction

SON SWUNG THE BARN DOOR open and shouted outside toward Maren, "Where is Earl?"

The girl was busy doing her chores while enthusiastically talking to herself and didn't seem to notice him.

"Maren!" he called out her name as he jogged out to her.

The girl startled, then stood up straight. "Huh?" she replied as she immediately began pinching her ear.

"Where is Earl?" he asked again. "He's not in the barn, and he's not with you."

The girl's eyes darted back and forth as she continued working at her ear. Finally, she answered, "That stupid donkey ran off on me."

"Ran off on you?" the boy said. He could hardly believe that the loyal beast would just run off. And if he did, he wouldn't be difficult to catch up with.

"Uh huh. After the festivities yesterday, he was gone from his post," she explained.

The boy thought for a moment. He knew the girl's words couldn't be completely true, but he didn't want to jump to conclusions. She always seemed so attached to the mule, and he didn't understand how she could let him go missing. "Do you think he was stolen?" he asked.

Maren looked upward in a thoughtful expression while she kept her hand on her ear. "Maybe," she said unconvincingly.

"Do you think it might have been your friend Micah?" he continued to probe.

The girl's thoughtful expression turned angry. "He's not like that," she answered. "He's a nice boy."

"How do you know?"

"Because he's like me. He talks about pirates, and reads, and likes to draw," she snapped.

Son could sense the tension rising in his young friend. He knew it would soon be difficult to continue the conversation if he didn't find a way to settle her. "I'm sorry," he said. "I'm sure he's a nice boy. I was just thinking through what could have happened to Earl."

"I don't know!" she shot back.

The boy paused to inhale deeply. "I was planning to go to the village tomorrow to sell toys. Instead, I'll go later today so I can ask a few people if they've seen him. Hopefully, we can bring him back."

Maren seemed to be jolted from her anger. She quickly scanned the field she was standing near and then swallowed hard. "Okay," she said, and ran off to finish her chores.

As Son watched her rush about the garden, he mulled over his conversation with her. A strange sadness rested on him that he didn't fully understand. As he turned to go back into the barn, he took one final glance at Maren and whispered a prayer.

Maren arrived in Laor tired, sweaty, and dirty from working in the garden. She had traveled at a near-running pace the entire way with a sword dangling from her waist, and it took longer than she had anticipated.

Once again, there was a tent encompassing most of the town's square, and she could hear laughter and merriment going on inside. When she looked around, she noticed that the tables full of food and dessert were gone but the man with the long, gray hair was in his usual place, looking over papers that were scattered about the table. She swiftly approached him and asked, "Are all of the sweets gone?"

The man looked up from his papers with sudden wide eyes and a half-smile. "Oh hi, Maren," he greeted. "No, the sweets aren't all gone. We have moved them inside today."

Maren wrinkled her forehead and pressed her lips together. "Why?"

"Because today is the grandest party of them all before we move on," he answered.

The girl felt her chest tighten with excitement when she heard those words. Eager to get in, she said, "Well, I brought a sword to give you." As she unsheathed it, she remembered how Faymia gave it to her before leaving for her hunting trip with Dulnear. It seemed special to her at the time, but now what mattered was not missing out on the festivities.

The man looked over the sword with interest before turning his eyes back toward Maren. "It really is a grand sword," he said. "But I'm afraid the only way to take part in our final celebration is by joining our crew."

Something about what the man said excited and worried

the girl at the same time. After reading so many books about swashbucklers and adventurers, she wondered what it was like to be a part of a crew. "What do I have to do to join you?" she asked.

"Well, you promise to come with us, and you help out with different things," he said.

That didn't sound so bad to the young girl. She squinted, pushed out her lips, and asked, "Would I have to come with you for long?"

The gray-haired man cocked his head to the side curiously and answered, "Why, yes. But it's a good life. There are lots of celebrations, new friends, and plenty of sweets."

The thought of abundant sweets thrilled Maren, but she didn't feel comfortable going off for an indefinite amount of time. As she pondered this, Micah appeared beside her, once again holding a tin plate filled with dessert.

"You made it!" he cheered.

The girl pushed her forehead into a pile of wrinkles and asked, "Made it to what?"

"To the best celebration of all," he answered enthusiastically. "Today is a pirate adventure show!"

Maren's eyebrows shot up. "Really?! I love pirates!"

"I know," the boy replied. "I told them about that and they're putting on the show especially for you."

"But they want me to join their crew and go off with them," Maren explained. "I don't know if I should do that."

"That's okay," Micah assured her. "I joined the crew and I know it's going to be great!"

Maren began to squeeze her ear as she thought about the offer before her. The last several days had been wonderful for her. She had been entertained, made a friend, and ate whatever she wanted without Son pressing her to make better choices. She was tired of chores and responsibilities, and Faymia and Dulnear were hardly around anymore. Her eyes widened a bit, and she asked, "Will I get to see Earl?"

"Earl?" the gray-haired man asked.

"My donkey," she answered, surprised he didn't know that.

The man's expression changed to a sardonic grin as he replied, "You mean *our* donkey." He then relaxed and continued, "Of course you can see the beast. Maybe even get to ride him."

"Well, then I suppose…" she began, before her attention was drawn to the man suddenly standing a few steps behind the table. She recognized him as Sevuss. His clothes were dark and fine, and his wiry hair was neatly combed back.

"Did you come to enjoy the pirate show?" he asked her with a tobacco-stained smile.

The girl didn't enjoy looking directly at the man because his appearance made her uneasy. There was something about his presence that made it difficult for her to look him in the eyes. "Yes," she answered as she continued to massage her ear.

"Well," he continued with a false kindness. "Since you're so young, we'll need to be gettin' a signature from your mom or dad."

A painful sensation turned in Maren's chest as she heard those words. She had no parents to sign the man's paper, so she answered plainly, "My mom and dad aren't here."

Looking put out, Sevuss replied, "Then I'm afraid you can't join us today. Go on home."

Struggling to get the words out, the young girl muttered, "Th-they're dead."

An edacious expression crawled across the man's leathery face. He reached over his assistant and pushed the paper closer to Maren. "I'm sorry to hear that," he said insincerely. "Go ahead and make your mark here, and you can run off with Micah to the party."

Dulnear stopped and looked across the landscape as the rocky crags and outcroppings to the west gave way to steep, rolling hills that gradually evened out as they moved closer to their destination. Though he was cool and confident in his demeanor, the tension in his neck gnawed at him. "This is taking too long," he lamented.

Breathing heavily from their quickened journey across country by foot, Faymia concurred, "I agree, and we've already lost so much time."

The man from the north inhaled deeply, pondering how they could make it across the countryside more expediently. As the stiffness in his neck grew, he asked, "How many days do the slavers usually stay in one place?"

The woman narrowed her eye and swallowed. Looking out over the gray and green horizon, she answered, "They only stay as long as they need. If they can get enough people to agree to go with them, they'll collect them and move on quickly. They're efficient and cunning, and I shudder to think about them in our little village."

Dulnear reached out and held his wife's hand. He struggled to suppress the regret he felt for being away for too long. Among his long list of regrets, this was fast becoming one of them. "We need to go faster," he declared. "And the next town is still a half-day's walk from here."

Faymia squeezed his hand tightly and began to speak before stopping herself abruptly. She sniffed the air several times and looked around. "I smell smoke," she said. "There must be a camp nearby."

The northerner wrinkled his nose and inhaled through it. "I smell it too!" he exclaimed. "Whoever it is, they may have a horse they are willing to part with."

The woman's keen eye spotted smoke rising in the near-distance. It ascended from behind the slope that ran off of the southern side of the road. "Over there!" she said, pointing.

They ran east a few paces to the edge of the path. Looking down, they could see a campfire with a handful of tents pitched around it. "I see four horses," Dulnear said, rubbing his dark, bearded chin.

Faymia's eye opened wide with excitement. "Let's get down there!" she said as she stepped off the road.

"Wait!" her husband warned. "Judging by the location of their camp, they probably do not want attention. I will approach them while you stay here."

Turning toward the northerner with a clearly annoyed expression, the former slave stated, "It would be faster if we both went."

"It is not our speed that I am worried about," the man countered. Since the woman lost her left eye to the northerner Searfain in Tuas-arum, Dulnear had felt particularly protective of her. He looked at the leather patch covering part of her face and confessed, "I only want you to be safe, my dearest."

"I can protect myself," she protested.

"I know you can," the one-handed warrior affirmed. "But I would rather if you did not have to."

Faymia stepped back onto the road and stood facing him. "I'll stay here, but I don't like it," she fumed.

"Thank you," he said, placing his massive hand on the side of her face, and he kissed her cheek just below the eye patch. "I will go and get us horses so we can be home before dark."

"I'll be watching," the woman said as she tapped the bow slung across her shoulder.

The man forced a smile and winked before turning around and beginning his descent down the steep slope that ran away from the southern side of the road. As he headed toward the encampment below, he reached inside his coat and touched the hilt of his sword. He also felt for another sword and a couple of knives that he kept on his person at all times. Though he hoped for a peaceful transaction, experience had taught him that one was not always possible.

Approaching the camp, his suspicion of its occupants grew as he noticed empty whisky bottles strewn about and a small wagon filled with fine clothing and odds and ends that clearly did not belong in a campsite. *Highwaymen*, he thought to himself. *Just lovely.*

Wanting to make his presence known without startling anyone, the man from the north called out, "Hello! Anyone here?" as he walked past the tents toward the fire. He could hear bottles dropping to the ground and, by the time he stood in their midst, the bandits were to their feet with swords and knives drawn.

"Who are you?" one particularly scruffy man yelled out.

Dulnear quickly and calmly surveyed his surroundings. There were four men who looked like they had neither washed themselves nor their clothes in a long time. The two men standing on the opposite side of the fire had a large log situated behind them as a makeshift bench, and the two others looked like they had been sitting on crates. "I did not mean to startle you," the man from the north apologized. "I was forced off the road by a landslide a couple of days ago and have not been able to find my way back."

The man to his left eyed him suspiciously. He had dirty-blonde hair pulled back into a thin braid and spoke through a cigarette. "Why are you so far south?" he asked.

Realizing that his size gave him away as a northerner, Dulnear answered, "I heard that the elk of these parts were particularly tasty."

"Well, there are no elk around here, *morian*; move along," the man insisted.

The man from the north did not appreciate the bandit's insult. It was especially abrasive since it was delivered in northern-speak. However, he maintained his pleasant demeanor. "Please," he began. "I would like to purchase one of your horses."

"They're not for sale," the man said. His jaw clenched and the grip he held on his sword tightened. "I told you to move along. Don't make me have to tell you again."

The warrior breathed slowly and deliberately. Calmly, he stated, "I have several pieces of silver. I would not expect you to part with the beast without proper compensation."

"Several pieces of silver," the man mocked. "Ya don't say! Well, in that case, let's talk." He then took the cigarette from his mouth and let out a loud, obnoxious laugh that ended with a sludge-filled cough.

Though his eyes began to show his irritation, Dulnear kept a cool head. "Okay then, what can I give you for the animal?"

The highwayman gestured to his companions, and they drew closer to the fur-clad northerner. "I'll take all of it, *tearang*. And then you will walk away, or we will use your enormous head as a footstool."

The man from the north's face turned into stone. He thought about Son and Maren in Laor, and the danger they were likely in. Standing in his way of them was an unwise highwayman with a penchant for northern insults. He peered at the bandit and declared, "I am sorry then. I will be taking what I please, with or without compensation. For your sake, I advise you to stay out of my way."

"And what, pray tell, will happen if we do not? Are you going to kill all four of us?" the dirty-blonde-haired man asked indignantly.

"Only if you are fortunate," Dulnear huffed.

"What's that supposed to mean?"

"It means that if one of you raises a hand, I will cut it off. If you attack, I will strike back." Then, in a motion far too quick to counter, the northerner plucked the sword from the bandit's hand and held its point to his neck. "But, even if you let me be, I am still going to cut that ridiculous braid from your head," he growled.

The braided man's eyes grew wide and he swallowed. The corner of his mouth began to twitch and he ordered, "Kill him!"

Dulnear turned the sword and slapped the man in the face with the broad side of it, sending him tumbling sideways. In the same motion, he backhanded the man to his right with an iron fist. The man fell to the ground, cupped his nose with both hands, and cursed groggily.

A third man rushed toward the northerner with a sword

ready to strike. Before he was close enough, Dulnear flung the braided man's sword at him, planting it firmly in his ribcage. He then felt a stabbing pain in his shoulder and realized that the fourth bandit had thrown two knives into it.

The warrior stood tall, pulled the knives from his shoulder, and grunted, "This was my father's coat!"

"Then you shouldn't have worn it to a fight," the bandit said from the other side of the fire. He then produced two more knives and cocked his arm back to throw them.

Suddenly, there was a whoosh and a thunk, and an arrow appeared in the man's chest. He dropped his knives and fell to the ground, clutching the arrow.

Dulnear pursed his lips and sighed through his nose. "I told you to stay by the road," he said.

"And I told you we were in a hurry," Faymia noted as she strode out from behind the wagon.

"Perhaps, but I was enjoying myself."

"Too much, if you ask me," his wife replied. "Let's get going."

"One thing first," he said. He then walked over to where the braided bandit was on the ground. "We will be taking two of your ponies, ne'er-do-well. You should have been more hospitable."

The man sat up, made an obscene gesture, then rubbed the growing bruise on his face.

The man from the north didn't appreciate the gesture. His nostrils flared, and he withdrew a knife from under his coat. "Thank you for the reminder," he scowled, and he reached down to grab the man's head.

The bandit kicked and pleaded for his life. "Don't kill me! Take anything!" he cried.

With a simple flick of his knife, Dulnear removed the dirty-blonde braid from the back of the man's head. He then tossed it into the fire. "You should re-think your life," he advised.

He and Faymia took the two healthiest-looking horses and rode east as quickly as they could.

○

"Woooo, rahhhh!" Maren whispered to herself as she watched the terrible Cutthroat Seamus the Fierce race across the ship's deck to do battle with Admiral Cole of the great ship Nollaig Moon. She could hardly contain herself as the play unfolded. Looking over to see Micah's reaction, she added, "Cutthroat Seamus is the meanest pirate on the sea!"

"He sure is," the boy responded. However, his face portrayed more boredom than excitement as he watched the players prance about, clashing swords and shouting taunts. "Do you think he'll ever defeat Admiral Cole?"

"Certainly," the girl answered confidently. "He wants that ship and he'll do anything to get it!" Suddenly, there was a flash, and a deafening boom as prop cannons began firing over the audience. Maren startled, reaching for her ears. When she realized what was happening, she began to laugh. "Boom!" she shouted, and looked back at her friend.

Micah laughed with the girl, then leaned closer to her. "I'm going to slip out for some sweets," he said.

Maren couldn't understand why anyone would want to leave at this moment. She looked down in her lap and realized that she had hardly touched the pie that sat there on a small tin plate. She took a big bite, then said with her mouth full, "Okay. Come back soon."

"I will," the boy said, then slipped out into the aisle and out the back of the tent.

"Pssssh!" Maren said as she used her fork to mimic the movements of Cutthroat Seamus as he fought against Admiral Cole and his crew. Enthralled with the play, she gave herself fully to savoring every sword clash, every costumed buccaneer, and every line uttered by the actors. When the play came to an end, she stood to her feet and applauded, as did the rest of the audience. It was the most wonderful thing she had ever seen!

As the cast took a bow and walked off the stage, the girl watched them jog to the rear of the tent and make their way outside. She was thinking about running out to meet them when a man's voice rang out, "Okay people! Let's make a line!"

Maren was shaken from the world of pirates and excitement. She looked around and saw sword-bearing men standing along the walls of the tent. The crowd that was so enthusiastic moments ago sluggishly shuffled into the aisles and began to queue up at the exit. She took one last bite of her dessert, set the remainder of it on the chair next to hers, and joined them.

The girl moved slowly toward the tent's opening. She could see cages, and men rushing about with torches. The cages sat in open wagons that were hitched to tired, droopy horses. A man asked each person their name, then he directed them to climb into one of the cages. As she approached the man, she declared, "I'm part of the crew."

The man looked down at Maren and said, "Of course you are. What's your name?"

"Maren," she stated.

"Well, Maren," the man said, looking over a scroll. "Looks like you're in the first pen." He then pointed toward a wagon that contained several women and her friend Micah.

The girl squinted at the wagon and rubbed her chin. The wonderful feelings she felt watching the play were quickly fading. "I have to ride in that?" she said.

"Well, we're all out of fancy carriages," the man replied as his face turned sour.

"Okay," the girl said, and began to take small, petite steps toward the vehicle.

Before she could get very far, the man shouted out, "Wait!"

Maren froze and turned toward him. "Yes?"

"I'm afraid you're going to have to give me that sword," the man said.

The girl swallowed. Even though she was willing to relinquish it earlier that day, she was nervous about parting with it now. "But, my friend Faymia gave it to me," she timidly protested.

"I don't care who gave it to you!" the man barked. "There are no weapons allowed on the crew."

Maren wondered about her decision to leave Laor. She thought about running off into the nearby fields, but was afraid. Slowly, she unstrapped her sword and handed it to the man. Turning back toward the wagons, she reached up to massage her ear and slowly walked over. She looked up into the cage. With the exception of Micah, its occupants appeared tired and joyless. Ascending the small staircase at the end of it, she took a deep breath and climbed in.

CHAPTER SIX

What's Left Behind

S ON WALKED DOWN THE ROAD, pulling a small cart behind him. It was filled with wooden toys and miniature versions of a trebuchet, catapult, and battering ram. He was always proud of his creations, and they sold very well when he would bring them into town.

Moving closer to the village, he noticed an unusual amount of litter in the normally tidy setting of Laor. There were bottles, papers, and even uneaten food strewn along the ground. It irked the boy to see such a disregard for common courtesy, and he wondered if selling his wares to a bunch of slovenly festivalgoers was such a good idea.

As he approached the town square, it looked as if a battle had taken place there. Rubbish was everywhere, and shopkeepers were tiredly picking it up and tossing it on a large fire that burned high into the cloudy afternoon sky. Others walked about searching for something, or someone, Son did not know.

When he saw an older woman sitting outside of the

pub, sobbing into her hands, he let go of his cart and slowly approached her. "Ma'am, are you okay?" he quietly asked.

The woman wore a gray kirtle that was clean and handsomely embroidered. The places on her dress where her tears had fallen looked dark and stained. She wiped her lovely face with a handkerchief and looked up at Son. "My family is gone," she lamented.

"Where did they go?" the boy asked.

"They left," she began. "Gone with all the rest to a place I do not know. They chose to be carted off with a slaver crew rather than stay here with their mother."

Suddenly a feeling akin to being kicked in the stomach by a mule came over Son. Waves of dizziness and nausea flowed from his head to his feet. "Did you say slaver crew?" he asked, hoping that her next words would inform him that he'd heard her wrong and that there were never slavers in Laor.

"Yes," the woman confirmed. "They've been here for weeks, throwing their parties, getting the townsfolk fat and lazy. You must not be from around here."

The boy's knees shook and felt weak. All the suspicious interactions he'd had with Maren over the last few days came back to him with agonizing clarity. The pie, the insistence on traveling to town every day, the tight clothing, and the loss of Earl; they all pointed toward what he should have seen all along. He cursed himself for being too preoccupied to realize what was happening. He'd sworn to watch over the girl and care for her, but failed to protect her from the snare of the slavers. "I'm very sorry for your family," he consoled. "I have to find out what happened to my friend." He then ran off to speak to a nearby shopkeeper who was sweeping broken glass away from the entrance of his store.

"Excuse me, I'm looking for someone," Son said, introducing himself.

The man looked exhausted. His apron was filthy, and his eyes were red with angst. He leaned against his broom and replied, "As are many today, lad. Who is it that ye seek?"

"A young girl, about yea high," the boy answered, gesturing with his right hand. "She has dark hair and wears an embroidered dress."

The shopkeeper scratched the white whiskers on his chin and looked toward the sky. "What's her name?" he asked.

"It's Maren."

"Well, I don't recognize the name," the man said. "But I do remember seeing a young girl runnin' around with a little boy over the last few days. She used to ride a burro into town until she gave it to those horrible slavers."

A lump formed in Son's throat, and feelings of dismay beat at his shoulders as he processed what had happened. "That's her!" he exclaimed. "I'm supposed to be looking after her."

The shopkeeper began to speak but quickly stopped himself. He drew in a deep breath, then said, "Many of our young people went off today, even whole families. I tried for days to get them to go back to workin' hard, spendin' time with family and enjoyin' the lovely land around Laor. But they just couldn't stay away from the parties, the distractions, and the feasts. They were slaves long before they got in those cages today. I only wish they would have woken up and seen it. All the slavers did was set the trap, then leave our town in shambles. I'd love to give that fella Sevuss a piece of my mind."

"Have you seen the girl since they pulled out?" the boy asked, interrupting the man's reflection on the past few days.

The old man looked away, then fixed his eyes on Son's. "I'm afraid I haven't," he said. "She was always with that boy, and they seemed keen to be in the thick of all the activities."

"How long ago did they leave?"

"Oh, I reckon about an hour ago."

"Which direction did they go?"

"East."

Son didn't know how he was going to do it, but he determined that he was going to find the slavers and get Maren back. He was angry with himself for allowing her to be taken, but an even greater rage was growing inside of him for her captors. "Do you have a horse you'd be willing to sell?" he asked, knowing that a foot chase would be futile.

"Oh, I suppose," the shopkeeper answered. "But I don't know what good it'll do ye."

"Just fetch it for me," the boy urged. "I'm going to go collect some things and I'll be back for it shortly."

Son bolted off as fast as he could, leaving his cart full of toys in the town square. As he ran toward home, he made a mental list of the weapons, clothing, and money he would need to find Maren and bring her home. He didn't care what it took. He was going to make it right—or die trying.

Son returned to Gale Hill. He was out of breath and his chest was pounding. He burst through the door of the house and ran upstairs, where he strapped on his sword and filled a leather pouch with all of the coins he had. He trusted that it would be more than enough to purchase the shopkeeper's horse and provide for incidentals along his journey. He then slung a bag over his shoulder and ran down the stairs to gather some items from the kitchen. As he did, he whispered prayers under his breath, pleading with the Great Father to help him bring Maren back home.

While the boy was filling his bag, he could hear horses racing toward the house. Before he had a chance to see what was happening he heard Dulnear's voice calling his name. He ran out the door to meet his friends and suppressed a tear.

"Son!" the man from the north cried out, dismounting his horse. He ran to the boy and embraced him. "You are here, and you are okay."

Faymia followed suit and wrapped her arms around him. "I'm so relieved," she declared. "Where's Maren?"

The tear that the lad had been suppressing escaped from his eye and ran down his cheek. As he looked at his friends' faces, the weight of his failure threatened to bring him to his knees. "She's not here," he muttered. "I'm afraid she has gone with the slavers."

Faymia's skin turned white and she looked as if she were suffocating. As if struck by a boulder, she crumpled to the ground and sobbed.

"No!" Dulnear shouted. "How long ago did she go?"

"Earlier today," the boy answered. "I was just leaving to catch up with them."

The man from the north growled, "Mount the horses, we have no time to lose!" He then ran into the house, darted up the stairs, and began rummaging through Maren's room.

Shaking, Son turned toward Faymia, who was still on her knees, weeping. He knew all that she had been through as a slave and vividly remembered the price they all paid to set her free. He placed his hand on her shoulder and swallowed. "We're going to get her back. They can't be that far off," he declared.

The woman took several deep breaths and regained a portion of her composure. She stood to her feet and looked at Son. "Even if we catch up to them, then what?" she asked.

"We'll buy her back," Son suggested.

"It's not that easy. Dulnear was able to purchase my freedom because Tcharron saw me as old and used up. Maren is young and healthy, and could be of value to a slaver for many years."

Son didn't know what to say. He only felt that, if he could find his friend, he would figure out a way to free her. "Then we'll—" the boy stammered.

Appearing in the doorway of the house, the man from the north completed Son's sentence. "We will do whatever it takes, even if it means slaying an entire slaver crew. Now, get on those horses before it is too late." He got on his horse and pointed it toward the road.

Faymia and Son shared the other horse, with the woman at the reins. "A man in town said he would sell me my own horse," the boy said.

"There is no time for that," Dulnear replied. "Just tell me what direction the caravan went."

"East," the boy said.

"Then east we ride—to bring back Maren!"

CHAPTER SEVEN
Wages and Cages

DULNEAR, SON, AND FAYMIA RODE east as fast as the horses would allow, and the rolling southern countryside flowed on either side of them like waves of angry green ocean. The man from the north was furious that the boy had allowed Maren to be taken by slavers but channeled his anger into determination to find her. Long past the village of Laor, he began to wonder why they hadn't caught up with the caravan yet. He signaled to his wife to stop her horse, then brought his own to a halt.

"I do not understand it," the warrior huffed. "We should have caught up with them by now."

"I've seen slaver bands before," Son added. "You can pass them at a brisk jog."

The boy's words collided with Dulnear with the force of an avalanche. He clenched his jaw and massaged his forehead. He was an expert tracker, yet he chose to charge after the slavers with no plan or thought. He got down from his horse and began to examine the road. He sighed and lamented, "There are no tracks." His face grew hot and red as the realization of his mistake set in. "Those wagons would have been easy to pursue, but we blew past them like fools!"

"How?" Son asked. "There are no crossings along this road until we reach Redbramble."

"They must have turned off a hidden path or trail somewhere. It is the only answer," the northerner clarified.

"Then let's race back and pick up their trail," the boy urged.

"We passed Laor hours ago," Dulnear chided. "They could have moved off the road anywhere between here and there. Besides, we have little daylight remaining."

Son joined his friend in the road and stared westward. His eyebrows pushed together and he swallowed hard. Nervously balling his fists together he asked, "What are we going to do?"

There were many angry remarks that the man from the north wanted to respond with. Instead, he asked, "Did the shopkeeper say anything that would be helpful to us? Anything at all?"

"Only that the slavers headed east," Son answered. "And that they were taking the townspeople in cages, like the ones we saw on our way to Blackcloth, I suppose," he added.

"What else, boy?" Dulnear urged. "Think. Recall every detail of your conversation."

The young toymaker shook his head slowly, squinted, and said, "He mentioned a name. I believe it was Sevuss."

The fur-clad swordsman straightened. "Are you sure?" he asked. "Is that the only name he said?"

"Yes. He said he wanted to give someone named Sevuss a piece of his mind."

"I suppose it is something," the man from the north

said. He then looked to Faymia, who was still atop her horse, and asked, "Have you ever heard that name?"

The woman looked to the distance in thought. "It sounds familiar, but I can't place it," she answered. Then, as if struck by the flash of a distant memory, she said, "Tcharron. I've heard Tcharron say that name before."

"So, your former slaver may know how to find this Sevuss," Dulnear observed. He had hoped he would never see the man again. His mood was growing more and more dark as the events of the day unfolded, and now that he knew he would be seeking out an enemy for assistance, he could barely contain his displeasure. He breathed deeply, then instructed, "We will ride until full-dark, camp for the night, and head toward Ahmcathare at first light."

○

Maren was shaken from her daydream by Micah's voice. "Looks like we're making camp here," he announced.

The wagons had formed a circle in a large clearing. Surrounding the clearing were tall trees that, to the girl, resembled stilted combatants waving swords above their heads. She was imagining them whispering eerie threats to her before her friend interrupted. "Where are we?" she asked.

Micah paused and rubbed his temple before answering, "I don't know. All of those strange, winding trails have me turned around."

Maren sat up straighter in the cage they were sharing. The others that had occupied it with her and the boy were already milling about in the circle. She remembered turning off of the eastward road and spending a long time traveling paths that were hardly suitable for their convoy. She regretted not paying closer attention to their route and was uneasy about having no sense of their location. "That sure was a great pirate show today," she said plainly as she massaged her left ear.

Micah's expression lightened, "It was! I had loads of fun."

The girl turned her eyes toward her companion. She thought for a moment, and then asked, "What was your favorite part?"

"Oh, I'd say the big sword fight with Admiral Cole at the end," he answered excitedly.

Maren squinted in response, then asked, "What was your scariest part?"

The boy pushed his mouth to one side and raised his eyebrows. "That must have been when Cutthroat Seamus's ship almost went down in the stormy sea."

Smiling, the girl continued her questioning, "And what was your funniest part?"

"Hmmm? What do you mean?" the boy asked with a confused expression.

"When did you laugh the loudest?" she asked, not knowing how he could possibly need clarification.

Micah's enthusiasm began to fade. "I guess when the first mate fell off the ship."

"What about the most exciting part?"

"Um, I don't know. I guess I didn't think that much about it," the boy explained. He then cleared his throat and stood up to make his way toward the cage's opening. "I'm going to go see if I can find something to eat," he said. "I'll see you later."

"Okay," Maren said, now sitting alone. As she looked around, her stomach growled. "Shhh!" she instructed the noise coming from her abdomen. Then she continued ruminating about the pirate show. "Watch your step, Mister Rumly!" she exclaimed in a hushed tone.

"Oh, I'll be fine. Just let me pull this rope out a little further," she answered in a deeper, gravelly voice.

"But you'll—"

"Stop pestering! Pshhhh! Ahhhh! Splash!!"

The young girl giggled as she recalled the scene. As she sat there repeating the dialogue and recounting the action, the world around her seemed to fade away and she was caught up in the salty sea spray, the clashing of swords, and the peril of a pirate's life at sea.

Suddenly, there was a metallic clanging sound on the side of her cage. "Come on out in the circle!" a man called out. "Important meeting!"

As she stepped out into the ring of wagons, Maren could see the man with the long, gray hair standing on a crate as the people gathered around him. "Over here please!" he yelled. "We need to discuss some things."

The young girl moved forward but kept herself behind the group so that she had space to herself. As the man spoke, he talked about things like terms of indentureship, contractual perpetuity, and consequences of abandonment. It was all rather boring and complicated so she chose not to listen and examined some of the other new crew members instead.

As she looked around, she noticed how unhappy they looked. They had just spent weeks celebrating, feasting, and being entertained, yet they appeared bloated, lifeless, and disheveled. It was a contradiction that she struggled to understand. When the gray-haired man said something about debt repayment and release, a small handful of villagers walked over to a table, signed something, and began to walk away, down the trail from whence they came.

Maren thought about going back to Laor. She missed her books and hadn't seen Earl as she had hoped. She also missed her sketch paper and pencils. She was excellent at drawing pictures and her bedroom walls were covered with her artwork. She decided to walk over to the table that the townsfolk had visited before departing and sign the paper so she could leave too.

When she approached the table, an irritable-looking man pushed a paper toward her and spoke words she didn't understand. He then sat scowling at her with his arms crossed. "Well?" he grunted.

The young girl felt anxious, confused, and embarrassed all at once. Her face went flush, and she aggressively massaged her ear as she stared back at the man. She then realized that she had no idea how to return home. Even if she did sign the paper, it would be dark soon and she would most certainly be lost. Her stomach began to growl again so she simply said, "Never mind," and walked back to the group.

As she returned to the center of the camp, she heard the man on the crate say something about possession and life-rights and then the group dispersed, with most of them returning to their cages. With nothing else to do, Maren returned to her cage too. She sat leaning against the back of it and, shortly after, a man came by and tossed a few loaves of bread inside with a couple canteens filled with water. One of the other slaves handed her a chunk of bread and she nibbled on it, but the growling in her stomach had subsided and her appetite seemed to have gone away.

As Son sat and stared into the fire dancing in front of him, he replayed the last several days in his mind. He could clearly see the evidence that he'd missed while in the moment. It deepened his anger toward himself, and he would have given anything to relive the experience differently.

As if knowing what the boy was thinking, the man from the north broke the night's silence. "If only we saw today with the clarity we see yesterday," he mused. His demeanor was less harsh than earlier, and he stroked his wife's hair as she slept on the ground next to him.

"But I did see something," the boy lamented. "She was always going into town. She claimed that someone had stolen Earl. Her clothes were even fitting too tightly. I was just too preoccupied with the things I wanted to get done to notice."

Dulnear took a deep breath and released it with a whispered word in his native tongue. He then looked at Son and said, "To notice another is one of the greatest gifts you can bestow upon them. I am very disappointed that this has happened. However, you are still rather young, and noticing is a skill which takes time and effort to develop."

"I only wish—" the boy began.

"Save your wishing for another time, boy," the warrior urged. "You cannot change what has happened. Focus your energy on retrieving Maren instead of wasting it on regretting your mistake."

Son knew that his friend was right, but it didn't make how he felt any easier. "What do you think is going to happen?" he asked.

"I do not know," the man from the north admitted. "But we will do whatever it takes to bring her home." He then paused for a moment. "I need you to know something though. I will not be pulling punches, nor will I stay my sword. Slavers care not for the lives of others. To them, people are simply a commodity to be exploited. They are the lowest of low. They seek only profit; their only interest is their own, and they will prey on the most vulnerable to get what they want."

"Then why is it not against the law to do what they do?" the boy asked.

"As long as people are not forced to sign away their life-rights, then what they do is legal. It matters not what means they use to dig their hooks into people, as long as they can persuade them to go with them by choice."

Son thought for a moment, again replaying the last several days in his mind. "When Maren came home without Earl, I should have insisted on checking out the festivities myself," he groaned.

"Perhaps," Dulnear answered. "Or perhaps you would have fallen into the slaver's snare alongside of her."

"That would never happen to me," the boy stated confidently.

"That may be true," the warrior said. "Or it may not be."

Trying not to take offense at his words, Son asked, "What does that mean?"

"It means that we are never as strong as we think we are," the northerner explained. "And assuming that we are strong enough to resist even the smallest of temptations only weakens our defenses against them."

Son pondered the man's words as they settled on his

shoulders. As he did, his thoughts began to shift, and he recalled his impatience with Maren. He remembered raising his voice and speaking harshly toward her. "Sometimes I wonder if Maren has any resistance to temptation at all," he speculated out loud.

"What are you saying?" Dulnear asked.

"Only that she seems to give little to no thought about caring for herself or her responsibilities. Her only concerns seem to be sweets and stories. It's no wonder she was so drawn to those festivals," the boy said.

"Ah, yes. She has always been drawn to the world of make-believe. I believe it is the graymind."

"That's just it," Son continued. "I can't figure out if I'm seeing her graymind or irksome behavior."

Dulnear snickered quietly. "You are seeing Maren. That is all that matters," he said. "She is unique, bright, imaginative, frustrating, and loved enough by the three of us that we would risk much to find her and set her free."

Son smiled and looked into the night. "I suppose so. It's just that she is harder to love at times."

The man from the north chuckled under his breath, "As are all of us, Son. As are all of us."

CHAPTER EIGHT

Open Sores

LATE THE NEXT MORNING, THE three travelers arrived at Lahald, one of the villages scattered along the outskirts of Ahmcathare. They had been there only a year before to purchase Faymia's freedom from the slaver Tcharron. The scent of the town dug into the woman's scars, releasing pain and shame that she had believed to be at rest since her marriage to Dulnear.

They approached the tavern where she once served drink and pleasure to loathsome men. As they did, the world seemed to spin around the former slave. She felt dizzy and her breathing became shallow.

Halting their horses outside, the man from the north noticed the change in his wife's disposition. "Are you okay, my love?" he asked.

"I didn't expect…" she said before wiping a tear from her eye. She looked at the large wood and iron door to the pub, then up at the window of the rented room above.

"You do not have to go in," the warrior broke in. "Son and I can speak to Tcharron ourselves."

As Faymia looked into the eyes of her husband, she experienced something unexpected. She looked at his broad shoulders, the hilt of his sword peeking out from underneath his fur coat, and the iron fist that Son had made for him when his hand was taken by his fellow northerners. She also remembered his resoluteness in doing what was right, even when peril was a certainty. She became emboldened by his example and replied, "I know I don't have to, my *layoak*. I'm going in anyway." She took inventory of her quiver and then dismounted her horse.

Son also leaped down from the horse and tied it to a post. He checked the buttons on his coat and felt for his weapon several times. "What should I do?" he asked Dulnear.

The man from the north replied, "Just stay behind me, and listen."

"What should I listen for?" the boy asked.

"Details of words spoken, metal being drawn, heavy steps. Let your surroundings speak to you and keep your hand close to your sword," he said. He then swung himself off of his horse and faced his young friend. "It is going to be all right, lad," he assured. "I will not allow any harm to come to you. Just be vigilant." He then turned toward Faymia and spoke. "And you, precious, are as brave and strong as they come. You could slay a hundred men if you chose."

The words her husband spoke had a strange effect on her. She felt both bolstered and like weeping at the same time. She pushed back the tears and gathered fortitude from his encouragement.

"Tcharron has no claim to you and no power over you," he continued. "You are not merely a former slave. You are beautiful, cunning, and powerful. Let us go in and see what we can learn about Maren."

Side-by-side, Dulnear and Faymia stepped into the pub, with Son trailing close behind them. The sounds and odors of the establishment threatened to overtake the confidence the woman had just gained. Knowing exactly where to look, she could see Tcharron standing at the end of the bar.

Son's fists curled into steel spheres as he followed his friends toward the back of the pub. There was a long bar counter there and well-dressed, cologne-drenched men stood around it smoking and cackling about matters he had no understanding of. His heart beat against the inside of his chest as if it were trying to find a way out, but he did his best to do as the man from the north said and listen with utmost vigilance.

"Tcharron!" he heard Dulnear call out in a deep, confident tone.

Immediately, the cackling ceased and all eyes were on the warrior and his bride. At the end of the bar stood a man with oiled, black hair. He wore a well-groomed mustache and beard, and reeked of an air of condescendence. He looked up with an annoyed expression. Then his eyes widened as he exclaimed, "Well, you must be kidding me." He then stepped away from his companions and approached the trio. With a broad, insincere smile he continued, "I never expected to see the two of you again. Did you come to return her to me?" he quipped. "I'm sorry to inform you that all sales are final."

The room erupted with laughter, but Dulnear's countenance remained unchanged. "You might say that we are passing through—" he began.

Before he could continue, Tcharron interrupted, "Then perhaps you should move along. You're not welcome here, unless you've brought me more of your northern gold." He glanced around for approval and the men at the bar sniggered as they stood up straight.

The hair on the back of Son's neck felt like needles as his mind rehearsed worst-case scenarios and proper defense maneuvers.

"You do not amuse me," the warrior continued with a dead expression. "We are simply here to ask a question and be on our way."

"Okay, mighty goat," the slaver jabbed. "What is it that—" Stopping himself in the middle of his question, he threw his gaze at Son. "Wait a minute. Who's the boy?" he asked.

Dulnear's calm demeanor began to show cracks as he clenched his jaw in irritation. "He is just a servant," he replied.

Son's mouth went dry as Tcharron and his men stared at him. He tried his best to listen, be aware, and stay calm, but he felt as if the room was reeling, and he willed himself to stand as still as possible.

The oily slave boss continued to examine Son from where he stood. Squinting, he asked, "Do you always allow your servant to carry a weapon?" and nodded toward the scabbard peeking out from under the hem of the boy's coat. As he did, the men around the bar shifted themselves into a semi-circle behind him.

"It is none of your business, slithery vermin," Dulnear spoke up, somehow standing taller and broader than before.

Reaching out to touch her husband's arm, Faymia broke

in, "We're looking for someone, and we need your help." All of the sound in the room seemed to fade into silence at the sound of her voice. "Please," she added.

Tcharron chuckled silently in amusement and turned his attention toward the woman. "Well, first you run from me, then your ogre-friend kills my men, and now you want a favor. You really are damaged."

The former slave took a deep breath and repeated herself, "Please. A child has been taken by a slaver caravan in the south. We must find her."

The man raised an eyebrow. "A child?" he said. "A child cannot join a caravan unless a parent signs away their life-rights."

"She is an orphan," Faymia explained.

"Then what is she to you?" he asked.

"We are her guardians."

The woman's words struck Son. He remembered finding Maren alone on the road. He vowed to care for her and keep her safe, and now they were all in peril because of his neglect.

"Not very good guardians," Tcharron cracked. "Did you sign for her?"

"No!" the woman exclaimed.

The slaver laughed, "Ah, such simple people you are. She cannot sign for herself if she has a proper guardian. What does she look like?"

Faymia cleared her throat nervously. "She is small, has long, dark hair, and is called Maren. We believe she is with a man named Sevuss."

Dulnear reached inside of his coat and produced a folded sheet of paper. As he unfolded it, he explained, "She is an excellent artist. This is a drawing she made of herself," and he handed it over to the man.

Tcharron looked at it and smirked. Walking back to the bar, he spoke. "A slave this young and lovely is worth more than ten like Faymia. It doesn't matter whether or not she was obtained legally." He then held the drawing over a lantern and set it ablaze. "You will never get the girl back from Sevuss. Go home and forget about her!"

Son could hear the deep growl in Dulnear's chest before anyone else could. He knew that the sound heralded blood and steel, and all movement in the room seemed to happen as if under water. He could see the man's left hand reach inside of his coat for the hilt of his sword, so he reached for his as well.

Tcharron's companions turned their focus on the man from the north as he swiped upward, catching the nearest man's shoulder and nearly removing his arm. The slave boss himself made his way behind the bar to gather knives to hurl at the warrior.

Immediately, four of the men were upon Dulnear. As Son moved to assist his friend, he felt a throbbing sensation above his left ear and there was a man in front of him holding a broken bottle. Instinctively, he chopped downward at the bottle, sending glass and the tip of one of the man's fingers to the ground.

Cursing, the man tucked his wounded hand under his arm. Before he had a chance to refocus, a swirling ball of blades and fur removed his leg from underneath him as Dulnear tore through the room like a force of nature.

Glancing toward the bar, Son noticed Faymia inching toward an unaware Tcharron. He began to make his way toward her, but the pain on the side of his head was now encompassing the top and back of it as well. "Here, little runt!" he heard someone yell before the edge of a blade narrowly missed his neck.

The boy turned to his right to see a half-drunk hooligan aggressively swinging a baselard in the air. The pounding in his head beat on like a kettledrum but he held his focus, knowing that the slightest lapse in attention could mean the end for him.

Quickly, Son advanced toward the man, which seemed to take him off guard. He backed up, nearly tripping over the chair behind him. This seemed to irk the man, and he lunged with his sword as he let out a snarl.

Taking aim at the man's extended arm, Son brought his sword down hard upon it, feeling the blade become embedded in the bone.

The thug let loose a deafening howl and jerked his arm back so hard that he stumbled over the chair onto his back, taking the sword with him.

Without hesitating, Son lifted the chair in the air and brought it down hard over the goon's head. As he lay there dazed, the boy yanked his sword from the wounded arm and ran toward the bar. Drawing closer, he could see neither Faymia nor Tcharron and his heart seemed to stop beating as the thoughts in his agonizing head went dark and despairing.

Suddenly, a flailing body flew through the air and landed behind the bar, releasing a deep, breathless groan upon impact.

Son and Dulnear arrived at the end of the bar at the same time, peering behind it together. The slaver-lackeys who'd stood so confidently before littered the tavern floor, and their boss was laying beaten and bloodied.

"Where is she?!" Faymia shouted while holding the tip of her sword to Tcharron's neck.

"I don't know!" the man insisted.

"Tell me!" the woman demanded.

"I never heard of her before today!" the slaver claimed. "It's not like we all share notes!"

Dulnear grabbed a bottle of whisky from behind the bar and took a sip. "I am afraid that this rubbish cannot help us, my dear," he said. "Perhaps we should tend to his wounds." He then began pouring the drink onto the open wounds on Tcharron's face and neck.

"Yeargh!" the slaver shouted before releasing a string of expletives that were so foul that some of the words were actually unknown to Son.

Unmoved by the man's pain, Faymia continued to hold her blade to his neck. "Think hard, wastrel. This is not what we wanted. You have brought this on yourself. Where is she?"

"I'm going to put a bounty on your worthless hides for this!" Tcharron threatened. "The three of you are as good as dead! Just wait until—"

Interrupting the tirade, the man from the north continued to pour the whisky onto the slaver, eliciting a fresh release of curses. "That is not the information we are seeking. However, I take comfort in the fact that you have an ample supply of drink here to pour out." He then nodded toward Faymia, adding, "Perhaps we need to go deeper."

The woman returned a knowing look and plunged her sword into the flesh along Tcharron's underarm, provoking a howl louder than any previously released. "Now," she said coolly. "Don't make us waste the rest of the bottle. Just tell us what we need to know."

Son could feel sweat running down his spine as he stood there. The heaviness he felt from allowing Maren to go off with slavers returned in greater measure as he watched a man tortured because of his own lack of diligence. He watched Dulnear dangle the whisky bottle over Tcharron's fresh wound and wanted to close his eyes. He was just about to turn away when the slaver shouted something.

"Ocmallum!" the man cried.

"What did you say?" Dulnear boomed.

"Ocmallum," Tcharron repeated. "He would know where she is. Or at least how to find Sevuss."

"Who is this person?" the man from the north persisted.

"He's the most powerful slaver in Aun," the man seethed through curled lips. "No slave movement happens here without his notice."

"Where is he?" Faymia grilled.

Tcharron glowered at the woman. "You think you're so mighty with your sword and your northern friend. You'll always be a slave, no matter how you're dressed."

Interrupting the man's ugly speech, Dulnear began to empty the whisky bottle into the deep, fresh wound beneath his shoulder. "That is not the information we seek," he added with gravel in his voice.

"South!" the slaver shouted with a shrill wail. "Near the village of Dorcadas. You would do much better to forget about the girl though. You will not speak to Ocmallum and live." The corner of his mouth then twisted into a sadistic grin as he caught his breath and he added, "On second thought, go. Please go. I look forward to hearing how he tortures you and ends your pathetic lives."

The man from the north flicked the bottle at Tcharron's bruised head, knocking him out cold. "Thank you for your cooperation," he added. Then, turning his attention toward Faymia and Son, he continued, "We must make our way toward Dorcadas with great haste. If we do not find Maren before a buyer employs her, she may be lost forever."

As the three of them left the pub and untied their horses, Son wondered if they would actually be able to bring his young friend home. "Do you know Dorcadas?" he asked Dulnear.

"I know of it," the warrior answered. "It has a reputation for being a dark place. It is not the type of village where one goes for a holiday."

Faymia mounted her horse. A look of concern began to manifest in her eyes. "I've heard mention of it before. When I was enslaved here, Tcharron would take trips to Dorcadas. I never knew why until now." She swallowed and added, "Even the name is gloomy and bleak."

A chill fell over Son as he mounted the horse behind Faymia. He knew that the only way out of this storm was through it, but he wasn't prepared for the journey. Thinking about the situation, he asked, "How will we find Ocmallum once we reach the town?"

"A man like that is proud of his wealth and power. He will not be difficult to find," Dulnear answered.

"Let's hope Tcharron isn't able to warn him before we arrive," Faymia added.

The man from the north stopped himself from

swinging his leg over the back of his horse and stood firm on the ground.

"What is it?" his wife asked.

"You have brought up an excellent point, my bride," he said. "Please wait here a moment while I go back inside."

"What are you going to do?"

"Tie up loose ends," the man said, and moved with a jog back into the tavern.

Son shivered at the thought of what Dulnear was likely doing inside the tavern. He was well aware of the man's poorly tamed violent streak, and the sound of thrashing about and mutterings of misery did little to set the boy at ease. He flinched when the door flung open and the northerner stood with the limp body of Tcharron over his shoulder. His voice trembled as he asked, "What did you do?"

"I thought we could use this piece of swill as a guide to find Ocmallum," the northerner answered. "He may also be useful as a bargaining chip to get the information we need."

"So, he's alive?" the boy asked.

"Unfortunately, yes," Dulnear answered as he bound the man's hands and feet and flung him over the back of his horse. "For now."

CHAPTER NINE

The Cost of Pie

"**P**SSST, MAREN. WAKE UP. MAREN!" Micah urged from outside the cage.

The young girl now had her own pen, and many more cages were added to their camp. Some were stacked on top of others, with makeshift ladders leading to their openings. The people came and went from the enclosures as they pleased, but they were not allowed to leave the camp. Guards were posted around the circle, and anyone trying to leave would be punished.

They were all given everything they were promised. There was food and the occasional entertainment, but somehow, it was soured now. Maren couldn't bear to eat the blackberry pie, and the chores were more demanding than the ones she did on Gale Hill Farm. She often thought of Son, Faymia, and Dulnear, and wished to see them again. They were much nicer to her than the slaver crew. Her only comfort was the presence of her friend Micah, who was now reaching through the bars and gently shaking her shoulder in order to wake her up.

"What is it?" the girl asked. "It's so early."

"They want you to get up and eat something," Micah answered. "There is a man coming to take you to Ahmcathare."

Maren's body shook from being jolted from her sleep and she urged her eyes to focus on the boy's face. Hearing that she was going to be taken to the great city was not sitting well with her. "Why am I going there?" she asked.

"You are being sold," the lad explained.

"Sold?" she croaked.

"Yes, to a man named Kugun."

Maren struggled to understand what she was being told. She massaged her ear and blinked. "I thought I was going to be a part of the crew. That we were going to put on grand festivities and pirate plays."

"I know, but you signed the paper, remember?" he reminded her.

"What paper?"

"The one saying that you could be sold," the boy said.

Suddenly, the sound of the other camp occupants became unbearable. The singing of the birds pierced the young girl's ears. A wagon wheel being hammered onto a cart caused her head to pound and a dog barking made her shoulders rise and her neck stiffen. She looked to and fro as if she were expecting to be attacked at any moment.

"What's wrong?" Micah asked.

Maren made a subtle rocking motion, back and forth, as she willed herself to focus on the boy's face. "I don't want to go," she murmured.

"Oh, it'll be all right," the boy assured her. "I'm sure Mr. Kugun is a perfectly fine fellow."

"Will you be going too?" the girl asked, still rocking.

"I'm afraid I won't be," the boy explained. "But we'll always be friends in my book."

Maren stopped rocking and allowed her neck to relax a moment. "Are you sure we'll always be friends?"

"Of course. You're my best friend," he said.

A smile began to creep out from the corner of the girl's mouth, but she suppressed it. Now fully awake, she felt hunger gnawing away at her stomach. "What's for breakfast?" she asked.

The concerned look on Micah's face turned to a smile. "We have loads of eggs, and brown bread," he said, gesturing toward the center of the circle where people were filling their plates before going off to find a place to sit and eat.

"Okay," Maren said tentatively. She exited her cage and followed the boy to where the food was being served.

Following orders to collect the eating utensils after breakfast, Maren picked up one plate at a time and slowly walked them over to the washing tent. All the while, she quietly told stories to herself about Smarmy Kidd Black and his pirate adventures, changing them a bit to include a trip to Ahmcathare. As she did, it dawned on her that she had not yet seen Earl, though it had been several days since they'd left Laor. Bending down to pick up a bent tin spoon, she heard a voice calling her name, "Maren! Just leave that and come over here."

Looking up toward the camp entrance, she could see the fellow with the long, gray hair waving her over. Standing next to him was an unpleasant-looking man watching her with drooping, squinted eyes. The girl wanted to comply, but couldn't refrain from completing her task. She picked up the spoon, ran it to the tent, and then walked over to the two men waiting for her. "Yes?" she said, standing before them.

"Now, Maren," the gray-haired man began. "This is Mister Kugun. He's a nice man and you're going to go with him to the city."

The young girl felt as if someone was pressing down with great pressure on her shoulders. She aggressively massaged her ear as she stared at the man from Ahmcathare. She studied his heavy, sagging features. His hair was dark, curly, and unkempt, and his large, round jowls were covered in stubble. "Stop playin' wif yer ear," he said in a gravelly voice, interrupting her examination.

Maren's eyes darted away from the man, as if she was caught doing something improper. "Um, what?" she asked.

"Stop playin' wif yer ear, er yer gonna stretch it out," he continued.

"Yes, Mister Kugun," the gray-haired man said, catching Maren's eyes.

"I think he was talking to me," the girl said.

"I know he was talking to you, Maren. And when he does, you answer with a 'Yes, Mister Kugun.'"

"Okay," she said, swallowing.

"Well?" the slaver said impatiently.

"Um, yes, Mister Kugun," she murmured, still tugging at her ear.

"I tink dis one is broken," the unpleasant man complained.

"Oh no, she's grand," the gray-haired man replied. "And she's young, so she'll give you many years of good service."

Maren didn't fully understand what the men were talking about, but she didn't like it one bit. She felt especially small and helpless, and wished she could go play with Micah.

"Den why does she look like dat?" Kugun asked.

"What do you mean?" the gray-haired man asked.

"She's not proper," he began. "Her hair is all over da place, she keeps whisperin' to herself, and she won't stop playin' wit her damn ear."

Maren felt as if the ground was swaying and the camp itself was shaking in a way that only she could feel. Her face turned red with embarrassment and she looked down as she willed her hands to stay at her side.

"She's plenty proper," she heard the slaver say. "I'll tell you what. Take her with you for a few days and if she doesn't work out, you can bring her back."

Kugun's upper lip curled and he raised one eyebrow sharply. "I know how you boys work," he snorted. "In a few days you won't be here, an' I'll be stuck wit 'er."

"Oh, no," the man with the long, gray hair assured. "We will be in this same place for the next fourteen days. I promise."

Maren continued to look down at the ground, hoping the man from Ahmcathare would decide to leave by himself. She could hear him rub his whiskery jowls as he considered whether or not to take her. She wanted to reach up to massage her ear for comfort, but she resisted.

"Fourteen days, ye say," Kugun considered. "I suppose. Load 'er pen up on my cart and we'll see how it goes."

"Excellent. You'll be very happy with this one," the man assured as he motioned to his associates to do as his customer instructed.

Within a few short moments, Maren was sitting in her cage on Kugun's wagon and they were making their way toward the path that led in and out of the camp. She scanned the circle to grab one last glance of her friend Micah, but couldn't see him anywhere. Feeling alone and vulnerable, she sat against the back of her pen and wrapped her arms around her knees, rocking forward and back as the camp fell into the distance.

○

"You're a lunatic," Tcharron groaned as he lay on the ground, glancing around the campsite.

"Be still!" Faymia ordered. The sky was gradually fading to darker shades of gray, and it was becoming more difficult for her to see what she was doing as she attempted to patch up the wounds she recently gave to the slaver. Dulnear and Son were nearby building up a fire, but it did little to provide the necessary light for proper first aid.

"Honestly, the three of you are complete nutters," he said.

"Pull your arm out of the sleeve!" the woman barked as she tugged at the coat opening.

Grimacing from pain, Tcharron grunted, "I can't. You cut too deep." He bared his teeth and went on, "Why are you even helping me?"

"Try this," Dulnear said from the other side of the fire as he tossed a full whisky bottle over to his bride.

"No!" the man shouted, and he reached over with his left hand to cover the deep wound on his underarm.

Faymia was amused by the air of helplessness Tcharron exhibited. After being under his total control for so many years, it was a guilty pleasure to see him in such a state. She suppressed a smile and picked up the bottle. Pulling off the cork, she handed it to him and offered, "Drink some. It will make this more bearable for both of us."

The slaver sighed with relief before grabbing the bottle and swigging down several mouthfuls. "You didn't answer my question," he said as he wiped the whisky from his bearded chin. "Why are you helping me?"

Helping him sit up, the former slave gently removed his coat and winced as she was able to more clearly see the damage she had inflicted on him. "Dulnear thought it was a good idea," she explained.

"Oh, the giant goat," Tcharron sneered. "He is a walking bad idea."

Faymia didn't appreciate hearing her husband spoken about that way. She released her support and allowed the man's shoulders to drop to the ground. "Sorry about that," she said insincerely.

The slaver let out another groan and coughed, "You did that on purpose."

"Yes, I did," the woman admitted. "Here, drink some more while I cut your shirt sleeve off."

The man tipped the bottle for another drink, then looked away from his wound while Faymia cut his shirt open to gain greater access to it. "You deserve him," he said. "How does it feel to be owned by a northern brute?"

Amused by his question, Faymia smiled and answered, "He doesn't own me."

"What?! But he purchased you from me—with an obscene amount of gold, I might add."

"Yes, and he immediately set me free," she explained as her smile grew larger.

"Why, in all of Aun, would anyone do such a foolish thing?" Tcharron asked. "Especially for an old, worn-out whore."

The words he spoke should have offended Faymia, but they didn't. She paused for a moment and thought about them. "He loves me," she finally answered. "And I love him. And true love is free to run away but chooses to stay."

Tcharron swallowed and for the first time, his face was missing its usual air of contempt. "A fine sentiment, but a fiscally foolish one," he stated.

"Says the man who has never loved," the woman rebutted with a sharp grin.

"Okay, so he loves you," Tcharron said. "But why does he think it's such a good idea to bring me along on this ridiculous chase?"

"He believes that you will lead us to Ocmallum's estate and help us get the information we seek," she said.

"The estate is not difficult to find," the slaver blurted out. With an amused expression, he continued, "Every peasant in Dorcadas knows of it. It is one of the grandest castles in the south of Aun."

Faymia squinted as she struggled to clearly examine the man's deep gash in the fading light, and the firelight dancing to the left of her seemed to be more of a hinderance than a help. "I'm afraid I may not be able to sew this shut," she explained.

"Wonderful," the wounded slaver snorted as he drank from the whisky bottle. "I'm going to bleed to death overnight."

From the other side of the fire, Dulnear called out, "You will be just fine." He then stood up and fetched a sword from the ground. He had been resting its tip in the flames until it was fully glowing red. "I will close up the wound for you."

He then walked over, took to one knee, and joined his wife by her side.

"There's no way!" Tcharron exclaimed.

"It will not be as bad as you suppose," the man from the north claimed. "And it would be better than dying."

"Wait!" the man shouted. He then drank as much whisky as he could in a single gulp before taking several deep breaths. Then, unexpectedly, his face bore a quizzical expression. "Do you really think you're just going to march up to Ocmallum's estate and demand that he give you information about this girl?"

"No," Dulnear said with a half-smile. "You are." He then pressed the glowing steel into Tcharron's underarm as the slaver howled out in agony into the night sky.

CHAPTER TEN

Ahmcathare

MAREN HUDDLED AT THE REAR of her now locked cage as Kugun navigated the narrow city streets of Ahmcathare with a horse-drawn wagon. Streams of people bustled alongside of them, and Maren feared one of them might reach out and grab her through the bars so she curled up as tightly as she could, keeping her arms and legs as close as possible. Their trek upward toward the city's center was often halted when another wagon traveling the opposite direction had to get by. Her new owner would curse at the other drivers and refused to stop and make room unless he had no other choice.

Most of the great city's streets were cramped and crowded, offering little of the grandness that seemed to be bestowed upon it from a distance. Its great spires and historic structures were breathtaking from afar. However, once inside the city proper, it was likely that one would find the filth and decay its defining qualities.

Maren buried her nose into the sleeve of her dress. The smell of the horse manure that filled the streets was overwhelming. There was also something else that bothered her about being in the city. It was something that was less obvious than the sights, sounds, and smells of congestion and manic activity. It was familiar in a way, but elusive.

Unexpectedly, there was a voice inside her mind. She recognized it immediately as the voice of her mother. She couldn't understand what the voice was saying, but the feeling she experienced was just as strong as when she'd heard her mother's voice as a younger child.

Maren closed her eyes and let the feelings wash over her. It dawned on her that the last time she was in Ahmcathare, she was with her parents for business-related matters concerning her father. They were returning to their home in Blackcloth when their carriage was caught in a rockslide along a mountain pass. She recalled, with vivid memory, the sound of stone crashing into wood, the horses stumbling, and her panicked mother trying to reassure her that everything was going to be all right.

She alone survived that day. After she crawled out from the wreckage, she felt the sensible thing to do was to continue the journey home by foot. After traveling for some time, she sat by the side of the road to rest until a boy from Blackcloth and a man from the north stopped to check on her. The boy took her in, and she had been well cared for by him until now.

"Out of the way!" she heard Kugun yell from the front of the wagon. She glanced left and saw a man hauling a well-stocked handcart. He was blocking the entrance to a precarious-looking alley. Once the man was further down the street, the horses began making their way between the cramped stone buildings, but not before her new owner gave the man a piece of his mind.

The noise of the crowd died down as they traveled further along the alley. Occasionally, Maren could hear Kugun curse as parts of his vehicle would catch the side of one of the buildings. She was tempted to reach out and touch the stone, but was afraid of what might happen if she did.

Eventually, they came to a place where the alley opened up to a large, rectangular space that offered access to the backs of a handful of shops and offices. As the wagon moved closer to one of those shops, Maren could see that there were many slender, winding alleys that branched out from that space, and the thought of getting lost amongst them gave her a chill.

Suddenly, Maren felt her cage jerk forward as the husky frame of her owner pulled it out of the wagon and let it drop to the ground. "Hey!" she yelled as her bottom hit the ground.

"Dis is where you'll be workin'," the man said as he pushed the cage up to the back of his shop, next to the rear door. "I'll git somethin' to keep the rain out of this cage until I get some space inside set up for ye." He then disappeared through a doorway saying something about being hungry.

As the girl sat staring through the bars at her surroundings, she could see litter being jostled around by rats. The air was stale amongst the backs of the enormous buildings, and it smelled of urine and rotting food. This was not at all what she imagined it would be like to be a part of the festival crew. She didn't like Kugun, she didn't like the city, and she wondered when she was going to get to eat again.

The alley was dark, and Kugun failed to return with anything to keep the rain out of Maren's cage. Each sound that came from inside the apartment caused her to sit up and anticipate a covering, or at least something to eat, but it was as if the man had forgotten about her there and was just going about his life.

"I'm hungry," the girl said to herself as a persistent gurgling emanated from her stomach. As she looked about, she counted the lanterns that were glowing from the various windows in the access space where her cage resided. "Five," she said out loud, and she felt a sense of comfort as their yellow flames cast a warm glow into the disgusting setting.

Echoing from one of the many winding alleys, Maren could hear a dog barking, and the sound of children playing and laughing. The sound brought a smile to her face, and great sorrow at the same time. She imagined the children coming to her pen and talking to her about pirates and books. "I like adventure books!" she declared to one of her imaginary new friends.

"We do too," the pretend boy said. "Especially Smarmy Kidd Black!"

Maren giggled. As she peered out of her cage at her new fictional pals, she noticed that her surroundings were much darker now. The barely visible sky was now pitch, and there were only two lanterns burning. She turned around and did her best to see the window to Kugun's apartment, but it was dark now too. Realizing that the man had turned in for the night, she swallowed hard, curled up, and massaged her ear.

Moments later, the sound of the playing children went silent, the dog no longer barked, and the final two lanterns were snuffed out. The darkness seemed to transform the dingy ally into something altogether different. There was only blackness now, and within the blackness was another world that teemed with terrifying sounds.

Rats gnawed on decaying refuse, the wind blew over a rusted scrap, an unidentifiable sound that resembled a dead body being dragged through the alley, and all of it seemed to be heard at deafening volumes that made it hard to discern if it was happening across the opening or right in front of Maren's cage.

Maren did her best to curl up even tighter. She kept her back against the side of the cage that faced the wall of Kugun's apartment. Though the darkness prevented her from seeing anything at all, she kept her eyes open. She shook as her surroundings took on greater life—and greater terror. The darkness seemed to take on a life of its own. It was no longer the absence of light, but a creature with twisted tentacles and razor teeth that danced through the air, reaching for a savory child to devour.

The girl now gave up on keeping her eyes open and closed them tightly. Through whispered prayers, her fatigue slowly and hesitatingly became greater than her fears and she drifted into a restless sleep.

○

"Here's some porridge," Maren heard Kugun say as he unlocked her cage. "You sleep too late. Eat up while I unlock de store."

The girl rubbed the sleep from her eyes and examined the bowl of porridge sitting in front of her. She was used to sleeping in her pen. However, the eerie sounds of Ahmcathare's back alleys interrupted her rest several times through the night and she was exhausted. She sat up, massaged her ear, and blinked at the bowl a few times. There was no spoon, so she carefully lifted it to her lips and tilted it so the gray gruel could find its way into her mouth. As she swallowed, she noticed a chalky, bland aftertaste that wasn't there when Son made her porridge. She didn't like it, but her hunger kept her eating more.

"Move faster, girly!" her owner yelled from inside. He lived in a small, two-room apartment at the back of his store. The building's rear entrance led to the dwelling, and there was a door to the shop from the room that served as a kitchen.

Maren almost choked when she heard the shout and coughed before taking the next sip. By the time she had finished all of it, Kugun was waiting in the rear doorway with nostrils flared and arms folded. "I'm done," she said as she exited the cage and brought him the empty bowl.

The man stared down at her as she tried to hand him the bowl. "What er ya doin?" he asked.

"Um, bringing you my bowl," she explained.

"Yer *my* slave!" he sneered. "I don't wash *yer* dishes! *You* wash yer dishes, and you wash mine too!"

Maren's knees shook and her head felt dizzy as Kugun barked at her. She froze as she searched her mind for words and phrases to respond, but came up with none. She just stood there massaging her ear, staring up at the man.

The man's face turned red and his upper lip pulled back from his crooked teeth. "Stop starin' at me and go wash the dishes!" he shouted as he moved back from the doorway and pointed toward the kitchen.

Maren leapt and dashed into the apartment. Having never been inside, she accidentally went into the wrong room.

"Da kitchen's over dere, girly!" her owner hollered as he pointed to the other room.

She turned around quickly, nearly dropping the bowl, and found a small room with a table, two chairs, and a counter full of dishes so dirty it was difficult to tell how long they had been sitting there. "Sorry," was all she said as she walked over to a sink filled with water and began washing her bowl.

"Now, you get dese dishes washed and den meet me in da shop. Do you understand?" the man said.

Without turning from the sink, Maren nodded her head. "Uh huh."

After he had left the room, the girl began to talk to herself in a loud whisper. "How did all of these dishes get so dirty? Have they ever been washed? Perhaps he needs to be schooled in cleaning up after himself. If he did, then he wouldn't need a…" She couldn't bring herself to say it. She signed to become a crew member, a helper, a worker maybe, but not a *slave*. The word sank deep into her stomach. Perhaps deeper than any other word she'd ever heard.

"Girly!" Kugun yelled from the shop. "I hear ya whisperin' somthin' but not washin'. Just finish da bleedin' dishes and get out here!"

Maren moved more quickly and spoke more quietly to herself. It wasn't the cleanest the dishes had ever been, but she considered the job done when they were all sitting on the opposite counter after a quick scrub with a sponge and a dip into the water.

"Now, I wantcha ta clean all da dust off da merchandise," the man explained as Maren walked into the shop. It was a small business with two large shelves that created three rows running from the front to the back of the store. Near the street entrance, there was a modest counter where Kugun stood to take payments for his wares. Behind it was a chair where he sat when things were slow. "My cousin is a blacksmith, and he makes all dese tools," he added.

The girl surveyed the shelves from where she stood, noticing that every bit of space on them was taken up by axes, hammers, augers, and gimlets. There were tools for holding, cutting, and hammering. Some she recognized from Gale Hill Farm, and others she had never seen before. They were poorly displayed, haphazardly strewn across the shelves, and covered in a layer of dust and dirt. "Like a tomb," she whispered to herself.

"What's dat?" Kugun asked.

"Nothing," she answered at a volume barely above the previous whisper.

"Well, take dis rag," the man instructed. "Dere's a big brouhaha comin' ta dis part of da city in a few days and I want dis place lookin' spiffy. Start in da front and make yer way toward da back."

Maren nodded in compliance but was unsure of the instructions and didn't want to ask for clarification because she feared stirring the man's anger. As he walked away, she murmured quietly, "Which front? The front of the apartment or the front by the street? There are three rows. Do I start at the front of one row and work my way back around of the other? Or do I get to the end of one, then walk back to the front of the next and continue there?" She was paralyzed with all of the ways she could get it wrong and incur the man's wrath so she stood with her hand on her ear talking out her quandary.

"Clean those blasted tools!" Kugun shouted from his chair behind the counter.

The girl startled to attention and grabbed the nearest tool, disregarding any instructions to begin at the front and work her way back. She worked quickly at first, but her pace slowed as the shape of each tool reminded her of something different and amusing. Some became swords and exotic weapons in her imagination, while others were assembled together to form fantastic machinations. Remembering her angry boss, she glanced over at the front of the store and saw him restlessly snoozing. "Psssh, ahhh!" she quietly breathed as she caused one of the tools to crash into another. "We need to clean the body," she muttered, then wiped the implement down with the cloth she was given.

Noticing that Kugun was now snoring, and the noise she was making didn't seem to disturb him at all, she allowed herself to become a little more lively with her play. "Look out for the metal pirates!" she said dramatically, yet in a quiet voice. Raising an unfamiliar object above her head, she declared, "The iron guard will stop them!"

When a customer came into the store, Kugun woke with a snort. Standing up immediately, he almost lost his balance from being jolted from asleep to awake so quickly. "What can I help ye find?" he blurted out.

Maren instantly stopped her make-believe and went to the back of the store where she tried to look busy cleaning tools. She spent the remainder of the morning cleaning, imagining, and doing her best to stay out of the shopkeeper's line of sight.

"I heard you like blackberry pie," Kugun said as he slid a piece over to Maren on an old tin plate. They sat at the table in the apartment at the back of the shop.

"Yes," the girl said, looking at the plate, then back toward the man's face. She didn't like the look of this pie. What she had at the festival in Laor was bright and full and smelled of fresh cream and berries. This piece was flat, the cream was runny, and it smelled as if the berries were beginning to turn. "Most of the time," she added, as she reached to massage her ear.

"Stop playin' wit yer damn ear!" he yelled as he slapped a fork down next to the plate.

Maren startled and let go of her ear. She sat up straight and swallowed as she slowly reached for the fork. The unexpected shout caused her hand to tremble.

"Why is yer hand shakin'?" the man asked with annoyance in his voice.

The girl wanted to say that it was because the man scared her, but she felt that would be risky so she answered, "I don't know."

"Well, yer a strange one," he replied. "Yer the worst worker I ever 'ad."

Maren swallowed again and took a bite of the pie. It was flavorless and felt like paste in her mouth. "I'm sorry," she said as she forced the bite down.

Kugun got up from his chair, turned toward the counter, and sliced a piece of pie for himself. Sitting down, he took a hefty forkful of it and shoveled it into his mouth. While still chewing, he said, "You've three days ta improve er I'm takin' ya back ta da camp. You hear me?"

The girl heard none of the man's threats. Instead, she

was fixated on a thin line of blackberry juice that ran from the corner of his mouth to the end of his whiskery chin. Pretending the escaping stream to be alive, she thought to herself, *Let's get out of this hole. It stinks in here!* and a smile escaped from the corner of her mouth.

Her boss's forehead pushed down into a chubby pile on his brow. "What er ya smilin' fer?" he demanded. "Do ye think this is a joke?" As he spoke, more juice came from his mouth and his exposed teeth revealed blackberry stains and pulp wedged between them.

The sight made Maren's earlier thought seem even more amusing, and a giggle escaped. When it did, she immediately noticed Kugun's lip curl and his eyes burn hot. She didn't see it, but she felt his large hand slap her across the cheek and temple. Her head jerked to the side and she felt pain radiate from there to the rest of her body. She caught herself on the table so she didn't fall out of her chair. As the room spun, she could hear the man howling.

"You disrespectful little brat! I git ye dis pie and ye mock me when I get cross! I'm not even gonna bother takin' ye back ta da slaver camp. Tomorrow, I'm sellin' ye ta da brothel!"

Maren began to shake. She didn't know what a brothel was, but she imagined it must be a place where people who aren't wanted are thrown away. She stared through the man in front of her and sat in silence as her mind tried to process the consequence of her giggle.

Kugun stood up from his chair, took the girl's plate, tossed it back onto the counter, and grabbed her arm with a painful grip. "Yer goin' back ta yer cage! If yer lucky, the ladies at the brothel will feed ye tomorrow!" He then dragged her to the back of the building, tossed her in her pen, and closed the lock with a heavy metallic *clack*. With face red and fists curled, he stormed back into the building and slammed the door.

Still smarting from the slap, Maren's lip quivered and a tear ran down her face. She deeply missed the kindness of her friends. It was late afternoon, and she had the evening and night to think about what was going to happen the next day. She was hungry, lonely, and in pain. After staring through the bars into the filthy back alley for several hours, she fell asleep.

The aroma of eggs, fish, and fresh bread filled the air. Maren could hardly open her eyes since her sleep through the night was once again filled with fear and restlessness. As she laid curled up against the side of the cage, she could hear the sizzling of the eggs as if they were a mere handbreadth from her. It then dawned on her that the top of her head could feel heat radiating upon it.

She jolted upright and was shocked to see a man sitting in the cage with her. He seemed to be cooking breakfast on a pan, but she could not see it, nor could she see the flame it rested upon. The morning was still young and the daylight hadn't fully broken through the last remnants of night, but she could see that he was old yet strong, and gray but youthful. Strangely, she wasn't at all afraid of him, for she sensed a certain undefinable quality of goodness about him.

"Good morning, Maren!" the man said cheerfully.

There was a peculiar chime to his voice, and his words seemed to be more felt by the girl than heard. As his simple greeting washed over her, an excellent clarity was present in her thoughts in a way that she had never experienced before. It was as if there had been an unnoticed buzzing in her head her entire life, and now it was gone. Wanting to say something, but not sure what, the girl exclaimed, "That breakfast smells delicious!"

"Don't look at it," the old man instructed plainly. "Just keep your eyes on me."

When he spoke a second time, Maren was drenched in strange sensations. She began to giggle for no reason, and her shoulders felt so light that she thought she might float up to the top of the cage and hit her head. Then her eyes began to water, and she cried. She wept and laughed, felt sorrow, joy, and everything in between, all at once. Feeling out of control, she started to fear. Just as she began to panic, she felt the man touch her hand, and there was peace. It was not simply the kind of peace one feels on a quiet afternoon picnic though. Rather, it was an absolute assurance that whatever she had to be afraid of was already dealt with, and her only part now was to appreciate it. She was about to ask the man who he was, but she already knew. Instead, she inhaled deeply, then asked, "What are you doing here?"

The man smiled and raised his eyebrows. "I was going to ask you the same thing," he stated. He then swept the hair from her forehead and said, "So lovely, so creative, so passionate. You don't belong in a cage."

The words moved through Maren like wind through a wheat field. Her lip began to tremble slightly, and she admitted, "I thought I was going to help with the festivals."

The old man tilted his head, looked lovingly at the girl, and sighed, "Oh, Maren, we both know that is not the reason you are here."

Maren felt ashamed for being dishonest with her answer. She could still smell the breakfast cooking in her cage, and she glanced around.

"Don't look at it," he reminded her. "Now, my dear, why are you here?"

Looking into the man's eyes, she swallowed and answered, "I wanted more."

"Hmmm. And what was it you wanted more of?" he asked, rubbing his chin.

"More pie," she confessed.

"You do like the sweets," the man said. "And how can I blame you? They're delicious! And what else did you want more of?"

Maren remembered the food, the music, and the pirate play. They distracted her from the responsibilities of the farm. They came easily and felt good, but she was beginning to see the dear cost for her decisions. "All of it," she sniffled.

"Thank you," the old man said. He then took a deep breath and leaned slightly forward toward the girl. "You have a beautiful imagination," he beamed with a smile growing wider beneath his beard.

"I do?" she asked.

"Oh yes, definitely. And do you know what?"

"What?"

"I gave it to you," he sang.

"You did?"

"Absolutely!"

Maren chuckled with delight at the thought. She had always been close partners with her imagination but had never considered that it was beautiful.

"However," the old man continued, "I didn't give it to you just for play."

The girl didn't fully understand what he was saying. She pushed her mouth to the side and squinted. "Then what's it for?" she asked.

"Oh, I love play," the man said. "I love make-believe and laughter. But to stop there is to only use a small part of the gift I gave you. With your imagination, you can create. With your imagination, you can solve problems. With your imagination, you can even bring things that are in my world into your world! It is far more than simply a means of shutting out the unpleasant business of the world around you."

"But how do I do those things?" she asked.

The old man stared compassionately at Maren for a moment, then answered, "You're going to have to spend more time in the world outside of make-believe," he answered. "It is here amongst the disagreeable, troublesome day-to-day where the best opportunities lie."

A tear began to make its way down the girl's cheek as the man's words sank in. "But the real world is so painful," she protested.

The old man sniffed and a tear ran down his own cheek, mirroring Maren's. "Yes," he said, "but pain is the anvil on which true greatness is formed." He then reached over and touched the girl's hand again.

At his touch, the sense of goodness that Maren felt about the man was magnified, but it was also accompanied by unexpected sorrow. It was a heaviness so immense that, had it lasted more than a brief moment, the girl was convinced that it would have taken her life.

"Do you remember what Son told you?" the man asked.

"That I'm part of your great story," she answered, rubbing the tears from her eyes.

"That's right!" he said with a grin. "You were made to be free, powerful, and heroic. Not a slave to plays and pies."

"I want to be heroic," Maren declared. "But I'm small, and I don't have any friends."

"Really? No friends?" the man asked.

Embarrassed for giving another untruthful answer, the girl corrected herself. "I have friends that have been very good to me."

"Yes, you do. They were a present from me," he said with a wink.

Maren sat and peered at the old man's face for a moment and thought about her friends. She remembered the way they cared for and protected her. The way they were patient with her quirkiness and loving beyond reasonableness. As she thought, an idea emerged. "I have to go back and free the other slaves from Laor," she blurted out.

"My goodness! That IS a heroic notion!" he said.

"It is?"

"Indeed. And do you know what?"

"What?"

"I believe in you."

"You do?"

"Absolutely!" the old man cheered, and he grinned proudly from ear to ear.

As Maren basked in the man's applause, the smell of breakfast grew stronger. She could feel her stomach rumbling and wanted to put it to rest. Quickly, she glanced down to get a look at the fish frying. She licked her lips, then looked back up to see the old man's face. To her bewilderment, he was no longer there. The man was gone, the food was gone, and the buzzing in her head had returned.

"I hope ye slept well, girly!" she could hear Kugun yell from inside the apartment. "'Cause as soon as I'm done eatin', yer goin' ta da brothel!"

For the first time, Maren noticed the filthiness of her cage. It disgusted her, and she felt compelled to escape from it before Kugun came out to sell her. She reached between the bars and yanked on the lock holding it shut. It did not budge, but neither did her desire to get out. She reached around again, with both hands this time, and pulled down with all of her weight, but it still would not open.

The girl stopped and listened for Kugun. It was quiet in the apartment, so she reckoned he was still eating. She examined the bars of the cage and wondered if she could squeeze between them. She stuffed her right arm through and managed to get most of her right leg out. Not confident in this strategy, she withdrew back into the pen.

Suddenly, she heard the sound of dishes being tossed onto the counter and she knew she had to make her move. She went back to the bars and squeezed her head through, badly scraping the back of her ear. Looking upward, she managed to get both arms and a shoulder out, and began to push hard to force her torso through. Her heart beat like a timpani drum and her hands began to shake. She wanted to groan as her belly and hips fought hard to stay in the pen.

Just then, the door opened and Kugun shouted, "Hey!!" as he jogged toward her.

Maren reached down, grabbed a handful of dirt and pebbles from the ground and flung them up at the man's face. As he spit and wiped his eyes, she pressed with her feet from within the cage and pushed as hard as she could with her hands from without. With one final effort, she got her body through, pulled her legs out, and scrambled to her feet.

"Why, you worthless imbecile!" the man roared as he reached for her.

She ducked under his arm and ran as fast as she could. The morning fog was still thick, and she didn't know which way to run, so she darted forward down one of the narrow winding alleys that snakes its way through the interior of Ahmcathare.

"I'll find ye, little idiot!" Kugun fumed.

She could see his silhouetted form searching just outside the alley's opening and did her best to make no sound.

"And when I do," he added, "Yer goin' ta wish ye'd never seen a blackberry pie."

CHAPTER ELEVEN

No Easy Way

THE SMELLS OF PHEASANT ROASTING and coffee brewing hovered over the campsite. Son sat staring at Tcharron as he devoured his breakfast from the other side of the fire.

"What's your story?" the slaver asked, still chewing on his last bite.

The boy startled, as he wasn't expecting to be asked any questions. After all, he had hardly been addressed by the man since they'd left the tavern. "Huh?" he blurted.

"Why are you part of this barmy lot?" the man said, rephrasing his original question.

Son didn't feel comfortable speaking to Tcharron. He had a feel and smell of menace about him. Looking around, he saw Faymia cleaning a knife nearby, and Dulnear was next to her enjoying a cup of coffee and a book. Their presence brought him a sense of safety so he answered, "These are my friends."

"Your friends?" the man snorted. "Don't you have boys and girls your own age to run around with?"

The boy exhaled and explained, "Well, they're really more like family. Dulnear taught me the ways of a warrior, and we work the land together."

Tcharron squinted as if he struggled to comprehend what was being said. "You're telling me that that ogre over there is your mentor?" Rubbing his chin, he continued, "The beast sets slaves free and helps wee lads. I don't even know what to say."

"He saved my life," Son added.

The slaver looked down at his plate and finished what remained without saying another word. When he was done, he set it aside and stared into the fire. Though his hands were free, his legs were still bound with ropes around the ankles.

"And Faymia saved mine," Dulnear stated, as if he was a part of the conversation the whole time. He got up from his place next to his wife and sat down next to Tcharron, sharing the log on which he was sitting.

The slaver looked at the warrior plainly, then asked with a hint of sarcasm, "Is that what you people do? Go around saving each other?"

The man from the north chuckled quietly. Inhaling deeply, then exhaling, he answered, "Life is meant to be lived alongside those who bring out greatness in you. You protect each other, care for each other, and inspire each other."

The shifty man looked over with a half-cocked smile and pointed out, "I have men to protect me but you keep maiming them."

"Those are not friends," Dulnear argued. "You pay them, so they owe you their protection. An entourage of lackeys is not the same as a clan of committed companions." He then cleared his throat and added, "And I would not have maimed any of your men had they not tried to harm me first."

Tcharron stared into the fire a little while longer. Grabbing a nearby stick, he used it to poke at the embers. "This has been my life for as long as I can remember," he confessed. "Am I supposed to go around looking after grannies and kissing babies on the cheek?"

Dulnear produced a large knife from under his coat and watched the slaver throw his arms up in defense. He reached down with the blade and cut the ropes from the man's legs. Once he had tossed them into the fire, he said, "Just start by doing one kind thing."

"Why would you do that?" Tcharron asked. "What's to keep me from running away?"

With a flick of his wrist, the man from the north released his knife through the air, impaling a scurrying squirrel and pinning it to the trunk of its tree. "I am sure you will do the right thing," he said. He then got up, retrieved the squirrel, and brought it back to the fire to skin and eat. When it was cooked, he shared it with the slaver and told him the story of how Maren bravely fought off bandits on the road to Blackcloth.

O

Dulnear, Faymia, Son, and Tcharron walked through the dreary village of Dorcadas cautiously. As they did, the townspeople either stared or scampered away timidly. Faymia was used to people behaving that way upon seeing the man from the north for the first time, but this felt different to her. There was a darkness about this place that caused her to wish she had waited where they'd tied the horses just outside of town. "These people are terrified," she observed out loud.

"They live under the shadow of the most powerful slaver

in Aun," Tcharron answered. "Fear and suspicion are all they know. They hang over this place like a damp fog. I've been here as a guest of Ocmallum himself and still didn't feel at ease."

A shiver ran down the woman's spine as she considered his words. She swallowed before asking, "Are you really going to help us find where Maren is?"

The slaver from Ahmcathare pursed his lips and looked at the woman as they walked side-by-side toward the town square. "I reckon I will," he answered slowly. "But then I must head back to clean up the mess you all made of my inn."

After saying nothing at all since leaving the horses, Dulnear broke in, "I am hungry, and I would not want to approach the slaver's estate on an empty stomach. Let us eat."

The town square contained a derelict, crumbling fountain in its middle, and was surrounded by gray, gloomy stone buildings that suggested Dorcadas was once a beautiful village but had now been abandoned by cheer and ambition. As they walked through it toward the nearest pub, Faymia noticed that all sound seemed to be hushed. She couldn't hear birds singing or children laughing. Even their footsteps seemed to make strangely little noise.

The tavern was large but mostly empty, with tables and chairs covering the floor in a haphazard manner. It reeked of smoke and filthy mop water, and the barkeep didn't bother to welcome them. They took their places around a table toward the back and Dulnear sat, as he always did, facing the door.

"What a hole," Tcharron observed, sitting across from the man from the north.

"'Tis but a shell of its former glory," the northerner agreed.

As they settled in, a barmaid appeared before them. She was young and pale and wore a bonnet to cover her thin, stringy, dark hair. In a quiet voice, she asked, "What can I get for you?"

"We want hot food," Tcharron answered abruptly and abrasively without looking at the girl.

Faymia looked at the servant and noticed her frailty, her worn hands, and the dark circles under her eyes. She was moved with pity and said, "I apologize for our companion's rudeness. What are you serving during this time of day?"

Without making eye contact with anyone at the table, the barmaid answered, "We have lamb stew warming."

With a kind smile, Faymia replied, "Excellent. We'll have four lamb stews and some bread if it's fresh."

Without saying anything, the young girl nodded and walked across the room toward the kitchen. As Faymia watched her, she felt a tear pool in the corner of her eye. She clenched her fist and looked across at Tcharron. Barely restraining her emotions, she chided, "We don't treat others that way."

With eyes bulging as if the woman had said something utterly ridiculous, the slaver began, "But she's just a—"

Raising her voice slightly, Faymia interrupted, repeating herself, "We don't treat others that way!"

Tcharron bit the inside of his cheek as he glared at the woman. Inhaling deeply, then exhaling, he answered in a sarcastic tone, "As you wish. Do I have your permission to order some ale when she returns?"

"If you do it nicely," she answered, still looking rather stern.

It wasn't long after that the barmaid returned with four bowls of stew and some cold bread. As they sat eating the semi-adequate meal, they discussed their plans for retrieving the whereabouts of Maren from Ocmallum.

"Do you think he will willingly give us the information?" Dulnear asked.

"I highly doubt that," Tcharron answered. "Even if he knows that her life-rights were obtained illegally, it's likely he would try to keep them."

Soaking his bread in his stew, Son held an indignant stare. "Why?" he demanded.

"Because a man like Ocmallum doesn't make mistakes, and neither do his associates. If he ran you over with his carriage he would blame you, and probably have you flogged for it," the man answered.

Faymia seethed at the thought of such an evil man. "Then what do you propose we do?" she asked.

"Our best bet is to let me go to the castle alone. I can bring it up in conversation with him and we'll see if he's willing to tell me," Tcharron suggested.

"Alone?" Son protested. "How do we know you won't just stay in there and turn on us?"

The slaver smirked, "You don't, kid. You'll just have to take me at my word."

"Okay," Dulnear broke in. "And what if your plan fails?"

Tcharron folded his hands and stared at them for a moment. Then he answered, "Ocmallum does not appreciate uninvited guests, so there is that chance. If my plan fails, then I guess we'll do it your way."

The man from the north leaned back in his chair and folded his arms. "Fair," he said. "Tell me about the estate."

The slaver's smug demeanor began to crack as he described the property. "There is only forest surrounding the estate," he explained. "But a wall defends it. There is only one gate, and it is guarded by archers. The castle is vast and cornered by turrets. Ocmallum rarely leaves the northwest turret, as it gives him the greatest view of the road leading in. He is terribly paranoid and is usually well-guarded."

An uneasy feeling began to creep up Faymia's neck as she heard the estate's description. "What do you mean by well-guarded?" she asked.

"He has a small army of slaves, soldiers, and warriors alike. If your plan is to storm in there, then you would do well to make other plans."

Dulnear leaned in and asked, "Does he sleep in the northwest turret?"

"Yes, he uses it as his office and his bedchamber. Everything his needs is delivered to him there."

"Why have a castle if you're just going to stay in one room?" Son mused.

"Like I said, he has a small army living there," Tcharron said. "Listen, I'm not exaggerating when I say that your chances of getting to him are very slim to non-existent. For years, unhappy family members and their hired mercenaries have tried to reach Ocmallum to get him to release loved ones. Their dead bodies are left hanging along the outside wall as a warning to others."

"We will do what we must," Dulnear stated. "Dead bodies do not frighten me."

Faymia nodded her head in agreement, but she was deeply afraid. Reaching under the table, she hid her hands, hoping no one could see them tremble.

Maren had no idea where she was. The interior of the city was a labyrinth of narrow, winding alleys that occasionally opened up to access the backs of shops, offices, and dwellings. Many of them looked so similar that she couldn't tell if she was passing the same doors or just ones that looked the same. The gray sky gave little sense of direction and seemed so far away, blocked by the gigantic, drab stone buildings. Her only hope was to keep moving forward, hoping that one of the alleys would eventually intersect with a city street and she would be able to find her bearings. Adding to her predicament, she knew that Kugun was in pursuit, and stopping to catch her breath was not an option.

"Ye can't run forever!" the man's voice called out, echoing off the walls. He wasn't moving very fast. He didn't seem to have the need. He knew the alleys well, and only needed to listen for her footsteps as she ran from hiding place to hiding place.

Maren nervously massaged her ear as she ran into an access area and hid behind a stack of crates outside a shop's rear entrance. She couldn't run inside and ask for help because Kugun owned her and she would just be returned to him. She watched as he lumbered into the opening, looking around for her. There were few other places to hide, so she had to dart into another alley before she was discovered. As soon as the man's back was toward her, she ran across the opening and into one of the passages.

"Girly!" Kugun yelled as he turned to see her go. Picking up his pace, he jogged in after her.

Maren's heart beat like a rabbit's as she sprinted through

the twisting maze of brick and trash, always with the sound of her owner's heavy gait behind her. Coming to another opening, she saw a handful of men unloading the contents of a wagon into the back door of a shop. As she hastened past them, Kugun yelled out, "Stop dat girl!" and one of the men reached out for her, scooping her up off the ground.

Maren bit down hard on the man's arm and he cursed as he let go of her. Without a moment's hesitation, she scurried off into another alley. She could hear the laughter of the man's companions echoing through the maze and Kugun's footsteps slowing down. Filled with renewed hope for escaping, she ran ever faster.

As she moved, she noticed that the air in the alley was getting more difficult to breathe. It grew pungent and thick. The buildings seemed older and taller, and the light was growing dimmer. *I'm running toward the city center*, she thought to herself, and dread began to set in.

The passageways grew narrower and the refuse was piled higher, making speed more difficult to maintain and stealth impossible. Squinting, she could tell that there was a section of decaying building that had spilled into the alley, blocking her path. Maren knew she had to turn around and head back in the direction she came, but now Kugun, and a group of men, were waiting.

She turned around and ran, hoping that her owner was still in the opening, apologizing to the men. Instead of running all the way back, she turned right at the first intersection of alleys that crossed her path. As she rushed through the damp, dim corridor, she noticed the sound of heavy running feet behind her. With lungs burning and knees aching, she ran even faster. Suddenly, she tripped over something that felt like a burlap sack filled with rot. Stumbling to her feet, she noticed something strange. There was a wall directly in front of her, and on each side.

"Dead end," Maren whispered to herself, and she felt weak all over.

○

Maren surveyed the dead end. There were trash piles taller than she was, and it reeked of decaying vermin. She could hear Kugun enter the narrow alley and knew that she would not be able to run past him to escape. She went to the corner of the dead end with the highest amount of rubbish and began to bury herself with it as she laid down.

As filthy rainwater began to soak her hair, she smelled something that triggered a gag. Looking around, she saw the rotting corpse of a stray cat, its tail nearly brushing her face. She wanted to move and hide elsewhere, but she knew it was too late. Her owner was nearby, speaking cruelly, "Girly, I know yer in here. Come out, come out, wherever ye are."

Maren said nothing. She concentrated on breathing silently, but it was difficult since the odor was so horrific and her body was attempting to heave.

"Come out, little one," he continued. "I have some pie fer ye. I'm gonna cram it down yer throat!"

The girl closed her eyes. There was no point in keeping them open since she was blinded by the garbage piled over her face.

Listening, she could hear the man rummaging through piles of trash, turning over crates and shifting old papers and empty burlap sacks. Then, it unexpectedly grew quiet. She knew that he hadn't walked away, but he wasn't making any noise. She curled her hands into fists and let the memories of Dulnear training Son fill her body. Her lip curled and her brow furrowed as she waited.

Suddenly, the trash that she had piled on top of herself was thrown off and Kugun was standing over her. His face was pale and glistened with sweat. "I'm gonna cut yer ears off, brat!" he taunted as he reached for her.

Maren quickly grabbed the tail of the rotting cat and swung it at the man, hitting him squarely in the face, scattering maggots through the air. He stumbled backward, wiped his cheek, and sniffed his hand. Immediately, he began to vomit, but still blocked the girl's exit. She stood with the carcass still in her hand, wondering if she should initiate another attack before the man regained his composure.

"When I'm done cuttin' yer ears off, I'm gonna kill ye, girly. The brothel is too good fer ye!" he yelled as he wiped his trembling mouth and stood up straight.

From the corner of her eye, Maren spied a broken mop handle. She knew she couldn't reach it before Kugun grabbed her, so she flung the cat at him as hard as she could. While the man flailed to keep the putrid remains from touching him again, she ran and grabbed the handle as quickly as she could.

"What, are ye gonna—" he began to say before being interrupted with a smack to the neck.

"Neck, knee, temple, foot, shin!" Maren shouted as she struck each of those places on Kugun with force and precision.

"Youch!!" the man groaned, stumbling backward. Rubbing his temple, he lowered his head, growled, and ran toward Maren, swiping her off the ground by her neck and slamming her against the alley's back wall, causing her to drop the handle, and she struggled to continue breathing.

In an instant, the girl reached around his arm with both hands and began clawing at his face, leaving bleeding scrapes and gashes under his red, drooping eyes. He dropped her, and she shot between his legs to get away. Kugun reached down, cursing, and grabbed her by the ankle, whipping her back in front of him, dangling her in the air upside down.

Face wounded and bleeding, the man snarled like a combatant animal. Huffing, he flung Maren against the alley wall to his left. The girl hit the wall hard with her back, then dropped to the ground, partially buried under rotting papers.

Maren coughed, trying to breathe, but was only able to exhale. The alley felt as if it were spinning and she was sure that, if Kugun didn't kill her, she would die from not being able to inhale. She forced herself onto her hands and knees and groaned as tears filled her eyes and panic clutched her body. From the corner of her eye, she could make out the man's lumbering movements toward her. She took the smallest of breath, and then another until she could stand up and face him. When she did, she noticed that his movements seemed strange.

Kugun took a small step forward, then another back again. His face looked as if he might vomit again, and he clutched his arm. He moved his mouth and Maren thought he was trying to say something, but he dropped to his knees instead, then onto the ground, and rolled onto his back, now grabbing at the front of his shirt. Finally he released a gurgling sound, and he just laid still with eyes wide open.

Maren ran over to the broken mop handle and clutched

it tightly. She then walked over to the large, lifeless body of her owner and stared at its face. The alley felt like a tomb, and the still silence seemed unnatural. She reached down and closed Kugun's eyes, then quickly retracted her arm. Massaging her ear with her free hand, she stared at the man's face to make sure he wasn't going to move again.

"Hey, poop-snot," she whispered to see if he would respond. "I don't want your pie." She then gave him a whack across the face with the broom handle. She jumped back, just in case he revived suddenly.

Wanting to make doubly sure that Kugun wasn't going to move again, Maren hit him again, this time causing a tooth to pop out and stick to his lip. Surprised by the sudden appearance of the yellow tooth, she dropped the makeshift weapon and ran out of the alley as fast as she could.

As Maren approached a familiar open area amidst the many alleys, she could hear men shouting to each other as they finished emptying a wagon.

"She got you good," she heard one of them say.

"If I see that brat again, I'm going to whoop her!" the other man yelled back.

She paused for a moment, considering her next move. Her hand shook as it reached for her ear, and her heart refused to slow down. Though she saw Kugun die, she possessed a lingering fear that he was slowly trudging behind her, still wanting to strangle the life from her.

She made herself small and watched, trying to make no sound. When all the men had gone inside the shop, she darted across the opening and into the alley that she believed led toward her owner's shop.

Zigging and zagging around crates and rubbish, Maren ran as fast as she could without looking back. Eventually, she came to another familiar open area. She saw her cage sitting next to the back door of Kugun's shop. Running through the still-open apartment door, she grabbed as much food as she could carry in a bindle, then dashed back out.

Still panicking, she ran down the alley that had brought her to the shop days before, and found herself out in the open street.

CHAPTER TWELVE

The Road is Long

MAREN SQUINTED AS HER EYES adjusted to the daylight. The hard, gray sky was clearly visible now and the world around her felt raucous and manic.

Knowing that the street ran uphill as it moved toward the city center, she turned left where the alley spilled out and made her way down, hoping it would lead her to the gates, and out toward the countryside.

Clutching her bundle of supplies from Kugun's apartment, she walked deliberately and swiftly along the narrow sidewalk, often stepping around other walkers, forcing her to travel in the street at times. As she did, the mixture of voices and activities toyed with her thoughts, causing her chest to tighten and her hands to tremble.

"She's a slave!" she swore she heard a beggar woman call out.

Passing a shop, she was certain that the merchant standing in the doorway was the man who had visited Kugun the day before. "Where's your owner?" she thought she heard him ask.

Avoiding eye contact, and any questions, Maren willed herself to keep moving forward. Moment by moment, her disdain for the great city grew, and she felt she needed to reach the outside of its walls or it would pull her in and consume her like quicksand.

Somewhere in the commotion, she thought she heard a voice shout, "There she is! She killed Kugun!"

The girl bit down hard, catching her cheek, and the taste of blood filled her mouth. A feeling, like a blow to her lower back, struck her, and she ran.

As her strides grew longer, the downward pitch of the road caused her to move through the air as if she were taking leaps rather than steps, and she narrowly missed a cart full of vegetables that was parked in front of a pub.

Eerily, a voice rang out above the crowd, "Get back here, girly!"

Maren glanced back as she fled with all of her might. No one seemed to be paying attention to her. Almost running directly into a large man sweeping the front of a shop, she weaved just in time and leaped into the street, coming face-to-face with a pony, then ducking and continuing her descent.

Many more leaps, a tumble, and a mad sprint later, she reached the city gates. As she did, she paused and looked back up the congested street. The crowd, the activity, and the unruly clamor continued as it always had, oblivious to the strange little girl in the filthy formal dress.

As Faymia crouched behind a large, fallen tree trunk, she could see archers stationed along the top of the wall around Ocmallum's estate.

"How many do you see?" Dulnear asked, squinting to make out what she was seeing.

"Three," she said. "But we have no idea what lies behind the wall."

"Hell," Tcharron said from behind. "Hell is what lies behind that wall."

"What do you mean?" Son asked, kneeling next to the man.

"I mean that Ocmallum has warriors from all over Aun guarding that place. Malitae from the southern islands, swordsmen from the north, and others that come from parts unknown."

Faymia's angst caused a ringing in her ears. The sound made it difficult for her to focus fully. She took a deep breath, turned to sit leaning against the log, and looked at Tcharron. As she did, the memories of being the man's property pressed down on her neck and she recalled the abuse, the shame, and the violation she'd suffered by him. An angry tear formed in the corner of her eye and the surrounding woods seemed to appear out of focus.

The slaver pushed his eyebrows down and asked, "Why are you looking at me like that?"

She wiped the tear away, swallowed, and said, "I only have one thing to say. I forgive you." Perhaps it was the distress of their predicament, or maybe it was the fatigue of carrying bitterness, she did not know. She only knew that, in that moment, she needed to say those words.

"What??" the man sputtered.

"I forgive you," she said again, this time more clearly.

Tcharron looked away for a moment, then met her eyes again, "You made a choice," he began.

"I know. I have no one but myself to blame," she replied. "But I need you to know that I release you."

The man's crouched legs seemed to give out and he fell back, sitting on the ground. His face softened, and the harshness faded from his eyes. He stared at the woman with an expression that suggested he was searching for words to say. Eventually, he murmured, "Thank you," and he turned his eyes toward the tops of the trees.

The woman felt awkward for saying the words, but relieved of the burden of holding them in. Holding her eyes on the upward-gazing slaver, she said, "Thank you for helping us find our friend."

"Well, I suppose—" the slaver began.

"If Tcharron's plan fails," Dulnear interrupted, "we will need to find a way into that turret without rousing everyone."

Faymia blinked and looked at her husband, shaken from her conversation. "What do you suggest?"

"Perhaps we can use the cover of night," Son said.

The man from the north raised an eyebrow and kept his eyes on Ocmallum's castle. "I think you might have something there, Son." He then turned and sat next to his wife on the ground. "How many ways are there into that turret?" he asked Tcharron.

The slaver brought his eyes back down from the treetops and thought for a moment. "Outside of Ocmallum's chamber is a vestibule, and there is only one staircase that leads up to it. However, the staircase lies at the end of a long hall which can be reached from three different doors from the inner courtyard. Since many of the men are drunk or otherwise preoccupied at night, you may have a chance of making it to the staircase without encountering too much trouble."

"And what about the wall?" Faymia asked.

"We would need to scale the side furthest from the road," Tcharron answered. "He is obsessed with every bit of activity that happens along it. If he is awake at that time, his focus will be there."

The woman was comforted that the slaver included himself when talking about scaling the wall. She asked, "And what kind of defenses lie along the wall at night?"

"Four or five swordsmen," he answered. "Mostly locals working off debts. The real metal is inside."

"Fine," Dulnear said, returning to a crouching position. "We shall go back to the village to buy hooks, ropes, and any other supplies we need. Then, we will return tomorrow to see if Ocmallum is willing to speak to you."

Faymia turned to survey the estate one last time. Her mouth was dry and her pulse pounded loudly in her ears. She thought about the man whom she had just extended forgiveness to and prayed a silent prayer that she and her friends were not being betrayed.

"Faymia and I will visit the blacksmith," the man from the north said. "Son, you and Tcharron will purchase some rope."

Son nodded in agreement but did not like the idea of being alone with the slaver. He set the boy on edge and brought upon him a feeling that could only be described as *contaminated*. "I saw a shop right over there," he said, pointing across the town square.

"Lead the way," Tcharron murmured, and the four of them parted for their particular tasks.

Walking over to the shop, Son noticed that the man was lagging behind, but he did not slow his pace. He entered the store and immediately began searching for a suitable length of rope.

Finding some, he grabbed it and turned to walk toward the counter. As he did, he nearly ran into Tcharron, who had silently caught up and was standing over him.

"Are you sure that's enough?" the slaver asked.

"I'm sure," Son answered with a start.

"Well, I'm going to grab another coil of rope."

"As you please," Son answered as he continued toward the counter.

"Hey, boy," Tcharron rasped.

"What?"

There was a pause, and the slaver continued, "You don't like me, do you?"

The young man turned around. He tried to measure his words carefully. He couldn't stand the man, but he knew that he was needed to find Maren. However, he could not lie. "I suppose I don't," he answered with an expression that was as friendly as he could muster.

"And why is that?"

Son knew about Faymia's past. He seethed at the thought of Tcharron using her to make money pleasing other men. He could feel sweat forming under his arms, and it was becoming an effort to keep a solid demeanor. "You behave as if you own everyplace, and everyone," he answered.

The slaver smirked and breathed out a chuckle. "I suppose I do," he said. "But if the alternative is to walk around with my head down, depending on others to defend me, then I'll take your accusation as a compliment."

The man's words hit Son in the chest. There was truth to them, but he didn't want to believe it. Digging for a retort, he said, "Well, you put far too much faith in your oily charisma."

"And you put too much in your war-happy friend," the man snapped back.

Son's face turned red and he could no longer keep his eyes from frowning or his teeth from clenching. "How do I know you're not going to betray us?" he asked sternly.

The smirk returned to Tcharron's face as he answered, "I'm still here, aren't I?" he began. "I could have run when you got ahead of me in the square."

The boy swallowed. He knew it was true.

"What's keeping me from beating you now and taking off?"

"My sword," Son answered.

"I could take it from you."

"I doubt that," he said as he reached one hand under his coat.

Tcharron took a deep breath. His face relaxed, and he continued. "Look, why don't we just buy this rope and meet back up with Dulnear and Faymia?"

Son's shoulders relaxed at the thought of being with his friends again. "All right," he said, and he let the slaver lead the way to the counter.

"All I'm saying is that your friend from the north may not be the best wagon you could have hitched yourself to," the slaver said as he paid for their rope. "You think I'm a bad person, but he probably has a kill list the length of Aun."

The boy was only half-listening. Instead, his focus was on the shopkeeper as they made their exchange. He was a lanky, balding man who eyed Tcharron in a disquieting manner. Trying not to be caught staring, he answered, "You're just lucky that you're not on that list." He then grabbed some rope and made for the door.

Tcharron took the other coil and followed him, replying, "Touché. And what happens when you rouse his anger? Will you be safe?"

"He's not like that," Son countered.

"As far as you know. Northerners are born and bred for only one thing. Sooner or later, you're going to see that sword of his turn on you."

The boy pursed his lips and stared straight forward as they walked across the square. He could see Dulnear and Faymia waiting for them. He tried not to think about what the man had just said, but a small seed of doubt was attempting to embed itself in his mind.

"Well then," the man from the north said. "I see you were successful, as were we." He then held up the two hooks he purchased from the blacksmith.

"Are you hungry?" Faymia asked.

"Indeed, we are," Dulnear answered for the group. "I suggest we return to the inn, have our fill, then turn in for the night. Tomorrow, we will execute our plan and move to retrieve Maren with expediency."

Happy to no longer be alone with the slaver, Son chimed in, "I second that."

"Fine," the northerner said. "After dinner, we will hire

two rooms. Faymia and I will stay together, and Son, you will stay with Tcharron. I trust that the two of you will do your best to get along."

"I'll do my best," the boy said dutifully. He eyed the slaver, hoping that the man was trustworthy enough to sleep in the same room with.

○

As Maren stood outside the city gates, she could see a great distance to both the north and south. The northern road stretched out until it became hidden by jagged hills and forest. The southern road seemed to snake around rolling farmland, punctuated by villages and ruins left behind by once-prominent monasteries and castles. She could feel an excitement growing in her chest as she envisioned herself far away from Ahmcathare and closer to her friend Micah.

A hunger nagged at the girl's stomach, so she fetched some bread out of the supplies she had grabbed from Kugun's apartment. She nibbled on it and walked toward the southern road with her eyes down, intending to avoid eye contact with any of the other travelers. "Don't look at me," she whispered quietly to herself. "I'm on a mission and can't be troubled by your bothersome questions."

As she walked further away from the city, her shoulders relaxed and her only concern became getting back to the slaver camp. She walked slowly but consistently along the winding road, spinning stories to herself about the great adventurer who freed the enslaved prince. Eventually, she stopped and reached into her bindle for another bite to eat. When she did, she noticed that it was getting more diffi-cult to see. She looked up and saw the gray blanket of sky dimming and the surrounding landscape fading to darker greens and deep blacks.

She walked until the darkness kept her from seeing the road very well and a mist settled in her hair. She began to grope around for a shelter that she could spend the night in and came across a cluster of trees that sat less than a stone's throw from the road.

Maren huddled under the branches of a hawthorn tree, pulling her knees up close and wrapping her arms around them. The night was dark and cool. Even though the ground was hard and it was difficult to discern her surroundings, it was far better than sleeping in a cage behind Kugun's shop. The air was damp and fresh, and she noticed the sweet smell of the branches above her as she closed her eyes. The faces of her friends appeared in her mind and she wondered about them. It wasn't long, though, before her head drooped forward and she was sound asleep.

CHAPTER THIRTEEN

Betrayal

"WHO ARE YOU?" A VOICE asked curiously. Maren opened her eyes to see a young girl standing in front of her. Yawning, she answered, "I'm Maren."

"I'm Athas," the girl said. "How did you get here?" She was fair-haired and blue-eyed, and seemed to display a constant expression of surprise. She wore a simple dress and apron that were not yet soiled from the day's chores.

"I walked," Maren answered, stretching out her stiff legs in front of her.

"Well, my mother told me that I have work to do but I saw you sleeping here."

"Where am I?"

"You're on our farm," the girl answered. "I have to go pull weeds."

Maren looked around and saw that she was not quite as hidden from the road as she previously thought. On either side of the cluster of hawthorn trees were rows of parsnips and radishes. She always hated pulling weeds at Gale Hill

Farm, but today the idea appealed to her. "Can I help?" she asked.

Athas shrugged her shoulders and answered, "Okay," before giggling and extending her hand to help the trespasser to her feet.

Standing face-to-face, Maren noticed how nicely combed the girl's hair was and that her clothes were appropriate for outside work. She glanced down at her own dress and, for the first time, felt that maybe it wasn't the best-suited outfit for garden work. Smoothing her own hair down, she asked, "Where should we start?"

The girl held onto Maren's hand and led her to the eastern edge of the parsnip patch. From there, a small house came into view, and they could see her mother inspecting another field in the distance. "I like to whistle a song and see how many I can pull before it's over," she said, and began whistling.

Maren liked the tune and started pulling weeds out of the ground between the parsnip rows. As she did, she counted, hoping to reach a high number. When the song was over, she shouted, "Nineteen!"

"Thirty-two!" Athas claimed with a broad smile.

Maren suppressed a grin and gave a playful, *Grrrrr.* "Hey," she said, then hesitated for a moment. "What should I do to be your friend?"

Athas paused and tilted her head. She took a quick but deep breath, then answered, "That's a funny question."

Maren felt embarrassed and reached up to begin massaging her ear. "I—" she began.

"You are already my friend," the smiling girl interrupted.

"Oh…oh yeah," Maren said, as if she had merely made

a slight mistake when asking about friendship requirements. Wanting to have her faux pas forgotten as quickly as possible, she suggested, "How about if you whistle again and we'll see how many weeds we can pull?"

"Okay," Athas agreed, and she began whistling the same lovely tune as before.

The two of them spent most of the morning tending the parsnip and radish patches, stopping occasionally to point out an exceptionally large weed or to determine who was more productive during the span of a song. Eventually, Maren's empty stomach got the best of her and she asked if her new friend had anything to eat.

"Sure," the fair-haired girl answered. "I was thinking that it was a good time for a snack. Walk to my house with me."

Maren was excited to see the inside of her new friend's house and she skipped lightly alongside of her, whistling the tune they had been working to all morning. When they walked through the door, she noticed how nice the cottage smelled. "Smells like bluebell and butterfly-bush," she commented.

Athas laughed, "That's exactly what my mother set out this morning!"

Maren smiled but did not understand why the girl was laughing, so she simply nodded her head, hoping it was an appropriate response. "Uh huh," was all she could say.

The home was well-furnished and had a large living area just inside the door. There was a hallway to the left, and just beyond the living area was a kitchen with a sturdy-looking table and chairs. Athas led Maren there and set out several slices of bread, some butter, and a bowl of jam. "I hope you like raspberry," she said.

Maren didn't say anything. She just reached for a slice of bread, spread a heaping dollop of jam on it, and ate it with large bites and little chewing. Her new friend also enjoyed the food, but with greater restraint.

Suddenly, a voice from the living area asked, "Who's this?"

Athas sat up straight when she saw that her mother there. She quickly swallowed her food and answered, "This is my friend Maren."

"I thought I told you to pull weeds this morning," the woman said sternly.

The young girl's eyebrows shot up, and she beamed, "She's been helping me. We've been having lots of fun!"

Athas's mother looked intently at the unusual girl from the kitchen doorway. After a short pause, she asked, "Where are you from?"

Maren felt uncomfortable and tried to make herself small by drawing her shoulders in. "Blackcloth," she answered.

"Blackcloth?" the woman said as her head leaned back in surprise. "What are you doing on the eastern side of Aun?"

"Traveling," she answered. She wanted to be honest, but didn't want to let on that she was a slave.

"And where are your parents?" the woman continued to press.

"Not with me right now."

Athas's mother closed her eyes briefly and sighed. "Well, Maren, thank you for your help," she began. "But when you're finished with your bread and jam, you're going to have to be on your way. My daughter has lots of chores to do today and she can't be distracted."

"But, Mother!" Athas protested.

Raising her voice to drown out her daughter's, the

woman interrupted, "You heard what I said. Finish your treat and say goodbye." She then turned around and headed outside to continue her inspection of the fields.

Maren took another bite of her food. This time, a much smaller one, and she slowly chewed what was in her mouth.

"I'm sorry," her new friend said.

"Okay."

Athas sat for a moment in thought. Then, the surprised look returned to her face and she bubbled, "Stay right here. I'll be right back!" She then ran out of the room and down the hallway.

Maren waited at the table, letting her bread sit in front of her for a while before taking another bite. She slowly massaged her ear and thought about the things she would have liked to say to the woman who just told her that she had to leave. She was just about to rehearse her words out loud when she was startled by her friend's enthusiastic return.

"I have something for you!" Athas proclaimed, running around the table to where she was seated.

"What is it?" Maren asked, swiveling her body around so she could see.

"I want you to have my old apron," the girl said. "It's still very nice, and will protect your dress."

Maren tilted her head forward and let Athas slide the bib's ribbon over her head. Looking down, she noticed that there were flowers embroidered on the steel-blue fabric. She reached down and gently touched them. "Squill," she observed. "I like squill."

"I want to fix your hair," her friend said, producing a brush.

Maren didn't know what to say. After all, her hair

wasn't broken. "Okay," she said, deciding to let the girl have her way.

Athas waited for a moment, then finally instructed, "Well, turn around."

"Oh, right," she said, swinging herself around so her friend could reach all of her hair.

As Athas ran her hairbrush through the tangled nest of thick, dark hair, Maren winced. Each stroke felt as if the girl was pulling handfuls of hair out at the root. She wanted to yell and get away from the instrument of torture, but she sat as still as she could, clenching her jaw until her face turned red and her eyes began to water. To make matters worse, the sound of the brush combing through her hair was akin to what she imagined seals vomiting to be like. Finally, mercifully, it was over.

"Thank you," Maren said through pursed lips, and she began to get down from her chair.

"Wait, I'm not done," Athas pleaded.

Maren swallowed and slowly inched back to where she was on her chair, taking another bite of her bread along the way.

The young girl then took a section of hair above Maren's temple and gently started to weave it. Unexpectedly, Maren enjoyed it and felt a sense of calm as the strands overlapped each other until they were one continuous braid. Athas then did the same on the opposite side of Maren's head until the two braids were brought together. When she was done, she brought out a damp cloth and gently wiped Maren's face clean. "There," she said. "Would you like to have a look?"

"Uh huh," Maren answered, moving her head back and forth. It felt strange to not feel hair on the sides of her neck, and there was a part of her that wondered if it felt this way to be bald.

"Here you go," the girl said as she produced a hand mirror.

Maren held the ornate mirror's handle and looked at her reflection with wonder. Still turning her head from side to side, she admired her friend's work and thought she looked quite like a princess. "Retrieve my carriage," she said, lifting her chin and experimenting with various courtly facial expressions.

Athas giggled and replied, "As you wish, your highness."

Suddenly, there was a knock at the kitchen window and a very stern mother was standing there.

Maren quickly put the mirror down on the table and slowly put the remainder of her snack in her mouth.

"I guess it's time to go," her new friend said sadly.

"Okay," Maren said through bread and jam. She then collected her bindle and walked toward the door.

As Athas accompanied her, she asked, "Can we play tomorrow?"

Maren shrugged her shoulders, gave her friend a quick, stiff hug, and headed out toward the road.

"Please draw me a bath," Maren said aloud to herself. It's what she imagined a princess would say to one of her servants. "And bring the tea to my bedchamber," she added.

As she walked south along the road, she spoke to each farm animal, shrub, and cawing crow as if they were subjects in her expansive kingdom. Stopping along the path, she looked out over rolling hills and endless stacked stone walls, wondering what it would be like to have dominion over all that she saw. "Rejoice!" she called to the fields. "Her majesty is here." Then, raising her voice to an authoritative bellow, she added, "And she is beautifully powerful!"

"Hello there," a voice came from the road behind Maren.

Startled, she turned around, and all the poise and dignity she was carrying fell to the ground. Before her was a husky, bald man at the reins of a horse-drawn carriage. Both the man and the carriage looked to have accumulated many miles. "Yes?" she asked.

"I know that you're in the middle of a grand speech and all," the man said with an amused smile, "But I was wondering if you could move out of the middle of the road so that I could get through."

Maren reached up and began to massage her ear. Looking at the man, but focusing mainly on his cleanly shorn scalp, she answered, "Okay," and continued to stare.

The man waited for a moment, then finally burped, "Well?"

"Oh, yes," she responded, and took small steps to the side of the road.

"Thank you!" the man hollered through his bushy, white mustache as he began to prod his horses onward. After inching forward a bit, he cocked his head and looked curiously at the girl. "Say, do you live here?" he asked.

Maren looked north, then south, and answered, "No."

"Where do you live?"

"Laor," she answered.

"That's a long way from here," the man said. "How did you get way out here?"

Maren didn't want the man to know that she was a slave, so she simply answered, "I walked."

The man looked confused for a moment, then kindly answered, "Well, I'm going to Redbramble. Would you like a ride?"

She stared through the man and thought about his offer. The idea of riding in a carriage was very appealing, especially after all she had experienced. "Okay," she answered, and began to make her way to the carriage door.

"I'm afraid the buggy is full," the man said before Maren could open the door. "You'll have to ride up front with me."

Tentatively, Maren climbed up onto the seat of the carriage next to the man, giving herself ample space between them.

"It's okay, I won't bite," the man said. "I'm Treyvin. What's your name?"

"Maren," she answered, still pinching her ear and examining the man's head.

The man prodded the horses forward again. Once they were rolling along, he explained, "Sorry about the carriage. I'm an abacus maker and I'm making a delivery. The old wagon is full of...what's the plural of *abacus*?"

Maren shrugged her shoulders, uncertain of the answer. "Abacuses?"

"Abaci?" the man suggested. "No, wait, abacoocoo!"

Maren suppressed a smile upon hearing the absurd word.

"I sure would like some abacocoa to drink!" Treyvin continued, laughing.

Maren couldn't help but giggle at the driver's humor. "Abacocoa," she whispered to herself.

"Look out, my horse is going abaca-ca!" the man chuckled as his face turned red.

Maren finally let loose with a belly laugh, repeating the words and holding her side. "You're funny!" she declared.

"Aww, thanks," Treyvin gushed. "But if you think I'm funny, you should meet my brother."

"Your brother? Where is he?"

"He's in the carriage sleeping underneath all of that abaca-ca," the man joked, and bellowed with more laughter.

Maren laughed too, but nervously, because she couldn't discern whether he was being funny or not. As she considered if there really was a man sleeping beneath a pile of abaci, she observed his smooth head some more, studying every contour and blemish.

"Do you like my head?" the man asked.

"Uh huh," she admitted as her checks turned red.

"Do you know how I lost my hair?"

"How?"

"I fell asleep in a sheep's pasture and they ate my hair!" the man said, guffawing.

Maren began laughing again and added, "They licked it clean!"

Treyvin slapped his knee and almost dropped the reins. "Hey, look!" he said in his best sheep's voice. "That guy's hair looks delicious!"

The young girl laughed so hard she could barely speak as she listened to the man's imitation of a hair-eating lamb. When her laughter subsided, she whispered the imitation to herself and massaged her ear.

"Say there, I noticed that you really like to squeeze that ear," Treyvin observed.

Embarrassed, Maren sheepishly took her hand from her ear and placed it on her lap, curling it into a ball.

"Don't stop on my account," the man said. "I was just thinking about giving it a try myself."

The girl pushed her forehead down, not knowing whether or not he was telling the truth. "What?"

"Well, it looks rather comforting," he said. "I'm going to give it a try." He then reached up with his left hand and began massaging his ear. "Why, this is rather nice!" he exclaimed.

Maren smiled, resumed squeezing her ear, and leaned back in the carriage seat. The two of them joked, told stories, and rubbed their ears all the way to Redbramble.

○

"So, what are you going to say?" Faymia asked.

"I suppose that I was in the area and wanted to discuss some new recruitment ideas," Tcharron answered.

The four of them were huddled in their previous scouting place behind the fallen tree. The air was cool and damp, and Faymia felt uneasy about their plan. "So, you're just going to walk up to the gate, tell the guard that you'd like to speak to the old man, and waltz right in?"

The man grinned and shook his head. "I have brought Ocmallum more fortune than any other slaver in Aun. He will be ecstatic to see me."

"Even so," Dulnear interrupted, "You need to have your story clear so as not to raise suspicion."

"Okay," Tcharron grunted. "I will say that I have ways to make the festivals more enticing and less expensive."

Faymia remembered the festival that lured her into slavery. She detested even speaking of them. "And how will you find out where Maren is?" she asked.

As Tcharron rubbed his chin in thought, Son leaned in, waiting for the answer with great interest. "Well?" he said, hoping to hurry the answer.

"I'll tell him that I heard the Laor fair was very inefficient," the man reckoned. "This should make for an easy movement into asking about your friend."

"Sevuss," the boy added. "I heard the name Sevuss when I was looking for Maren."

The slaver smirked. "So, your friend was taken by that old piece of flotsam. I don't know where he makes camp, but it should be easy enough to find out once I'm inside."

"Good," the man from the north said. "And when you have gathered all of the information we need, you will meet us at the tavern."

"Yes, I'll meet you at that wretched little pub. Then I must get back to my own," he said.

Knowing that the plan was about to be put in motion, Faymia's hands began to sweat and her heart seemed to be causing her entire chest to flutter. She tried to come up with one more question that might cause her to feel more at ease, but none came to her. "All right," she said. "Go. And be careful."

Tcharron looked at his three companions and began to say something before cutting himself off. He pushed the corners of his mouth up into an uncertain grin. "See you later," he said, and made his way through the brush toward the path leading to the castle gate.

Faymia, Dulnear, and Son crouched, peeking over the giant tree trunk, waiting for the slaver to arrive at the portcullis. Though afraid and tense, the woman felt an excitement growing in her as she thought about reuniting with Maren.

Suddenly, a voice barked, "Identify yourself!"

Faymia could see that Tcharron had reached the castle, and the gate guard stationed on the wall above and to the right of the gate was calling down to him.

"Raise the portcullis," the slaver instructed. "It is Tcharron of Teiparmhain here to see Ocmallum."

"What business do you have?" the guard asked.

"I wish to speak to him about the festivals," the man explained. "Just tell him that I'm here. He'll be glad to see me," he declared with his usual cockiness.

Just then, a voice boomed out from the northwest turret, "Tcharron! What an unexpected surprise!"

Faymia could see that the turret had an open window and a long-haired, yet well-groomed, man leaned out of it. "That is the horrible dung of a man," she heard Dulnear whisper in her ear.

"Ocmallum!" Tcharron called with a great smile on his face.

"What brings you all the way to Dorcadas?" the slaver king asked. "Do you need to borrow some money?" he added with a deep-throated laugh.

Tcharron's expression changed at the man's jest and he took a small step back. "No, sir," he said. "I was just nearby and wanted to share some new ideas that I had to procure our product at a lower cost."

Faymia's stomach began to turn. She believed she had made a grievous error and all that she could do now was watch it play out, and pray.

"Then why do you look like you were robbed on the way to my estate?" the old man asked.

Tcharron looked away for a moment, then back up

toward the man in the turret. "You're very observant, old friend," he began. "I was ambushed by bandits outside of town. They took everything. They beat me, took my silver, and rode off in my carriage."

"We should go now," the man from the north said quietly.

"No, wait just a moment," the woman pleaded.

"Why didn't you just say so?" Ocmallum asked from the window.

"Well, you know how I like to keep up appearances," Tcharron answered. "I couldn't show up here asking for a few coins to get home."

"Don't be absurd!" the man shouted. "You're my top associate. I'll send a servant down to help you get cleaned up."

"Thank you, sir!" Tcharron shouted back with a smile.

"Oh, just one thing," Ocmallum said, gesturing.

"What is that?"

"Why didn't I see you on the road?"

Tcharron swallowed and asked, "What do you mean?"

"It's just that I didn't see you coming down the road. You seemed to just appear at my gate."

Tcharron looked back toward the woods from which he came, and at the path that led to the gate. "I—" he began to say when an arrow pierced his chest, and then another, and another, until he fell to his knees. He looked up at the gate guard who was drawing another arrow. He then fell sideways, motionless.

Faymia crouched, paralyzed. She was so focused on remaining silent that she hardly noticed Dulnear scoop her up and run through the forest with his shoulder down and sword drawn. The world was spinning, and it felt as if Maren was lost forever.

Maren walked away from Redbramble, smiling. She enjoyed the company of Treyvin and whispered some of the humorous things he had said, laughing an airy, quiet laugh as she recalled him saying them.

She walked along the right side of the road because she knew that the path to the slaver camp was there. She remembered it being well concealed, and had to take regular breaks from entertaining herself to scan the brush for an opening. It was already growing late, though, and the gray, cheerless sky was getting darker.

"Be free!" she said in a dramatic yet hushed voice. "I've come to get you out of here!"

Maren imagined approaching the slaver camp with such authority that all of the slavers trembled in dismay and released the slaves out of fear for her terrible retribution. As she stomped along in the ever-increasing darkness, she felt her right foot fall into a shallow rut and she tripped and fell to the ground.

Starting to get back to her feet, she realized that the rut led away from the road and that it must have been the path to the slaver camp. She stood up, peered into the woods, and could see flickering light from a fire in the distance. "This is it!" she said to herself, and curled her upper lip in defiance.

Maren silently made her way down the winding path toward the camp. With each step, she did her best to quiet her breathing and find an approach that would keep her hidden. Drawing closer, she could see that there were fewer slaves than before. Some looked to be bustling about, cleaning up after a meal. Others seemed to be reclining in their cages. Peeking in closer, she noticed a young boy roaming about with a pastry.

"Micah," she said to herself, and crept out into the clearing to speak to him.

Kneeling just behind one of the cages that encircled the camp, she waited for him to walk by. The fire burned high, illuminating the clearing, and she feared that she would be discovered before catching his attention.

Finally, as he happened to walk by, the girl whispered, "Psssst. Micah."

The boy looked around with a confused look on his face before taking a bite of his pastry.

"Micah," she said again, just a little louder.

"Who's there?" the boy asked with a muffled croak.

Maren stood up straight and sidestepped from behind the cage. "It's me, Maren," she announced quietly.

"Maren?" the boy said, dropping his dessert. "What are you doing here?"

"I came to get you out," she declared, gesturing for him to come to her.

Micah ran closer, cocked his fist back, and punched the young girl in the nose, causing her to stumble backwards as blood began to flow. While she was still stunned, he grabbed her by the hair and dragged her around to the front of the pen, throwing her in, slamming the door, and barring it shut. "You are terribly foolish!" he crowed. "I can't believe you came here."

The world spun as Maren tried to understand what just happened. All of the bluster and confidence she carried with her earlier was gone. "Micah!" she cried. "Why did you do that?"

Suddenly appearing next to the boy was Sevuss. His gray-and-ginger hair was out of place and his clothing looked hastily thrown on. Putting his arm around the boy, he said, "Well done, son. You've caught a runaway!"

Micah beamed and replied, "Thank you, Father. I'm sure Mister Kugun will be glad we caught her."

Maren had difficulty processing what she had just seen. The feeling of betrayal was like a dagger to her back, and she struggled to speak. "Kugun is dead," she muttered.

"What?!" Sevuss barked. "What do you mean?"

"He d-died," the girl stuttered.

The man stared stony-faced at the girl. Then, a wiry smile crept over his face. "I get to sell you again!" he declared. "That will make up for that stupid mule running off!"

Maren shuddered at the thought of being sold again. She wrapped her arms around her knees and began to gently rock back and forth. Finally, the last part of the man's statement dawned on her. "Mule? Do you mean Earl?"

"Yes, Earl, you dullard!" Micah broke in. "He was supposed to be mine, but he ran away days after you signed him over to us."

Maren reached for her ear and began to squeeze it as she continued to rock. Though words flew through her mind like autumn leaves on a windy day, she couldn't speak a single one of them.

"Here's what's going to happen, little girl," Sevuss announced. "There's a whole party of buyers coming in the morning. Before they get here, I'm going to brand you like I should have branded that donkey. If you try running from them, there'll be nowhere to hide. No one is going to help a branded slave. You'll wear that scar for life!"

"Father, can I watch?" Micah asked.

Maren couldn't hear the man's answer. The thoughts continued to swirl in her head and she swayed forward and back, occasionally snatching a random word or two to whisper to herself in an attempt to bring some sort of comfort from the agony that awaited her the next day.

CHAPTER FOURTEEN

Ocmallum

DULNEAR STARED UP AT THE courtyard wall that ran along the back side of Ocmallum's estate. There were torches placed along the top of the wall, but the darkness seemed to crowd out the scant light they provided. "Still only three guards along the wall," he said in a half-whisper. "I should be able to dispense with them with little effort."

"How will you get up there?" Faymia asked.

The man from the north squinted and pointed toward the barely lit barrier. "I shall climb up the east wall, close to the turret. The merlons are well spaced, and it is darkest there. I noticed that the guard patrolling that place does not like to go too far into the darkness." He then quietly marched toward the wall with Faymia and Son in tow.

"What will you do once you're inside?" Son asked.

"Tcharron said that there are three doorways that provide entry into the hallway which leads to the staircase up to Ocmallum's chamber," Dulnear began as he recalled the slaver's description. "I only need to make it across the courtyard and into the northwest door. Once I am there, I need only to defeat his guards and demand the location of Sevuss's camp."

"But you don't know what's inside the courtyard," Faymia said. "There could be an army waiting in there."

The man from the north took a deep breath and paused for a moment. He knew she was right, but was willing to risk much to bring Maren home. "I will be very careful," he assured her. Half-smiling, he added, "I promise not to try to fight them all."

Once positioned in front of the darkest span of the east wall, the warrior waited for the guard to be at a good distance before tossing his hook up to the battlement. Giving it a quick tug, he and the two others pressed themselves tightly against the wall and waited for the guard to make his round toward them, and back toward the south wall again. Once the path was clear, he ascended quickly but awkwardly to the top and crouched unseen in the blackness. *Oh, to have two hands again*, he mused.

From his position, he could see fires burning and men crowded around them. The warm, orange light danced across them and it was difficult to tell whether they were soldiers, servants, or something else. However, once inside, he would only be a short distance from the doorway leading to Ocmallum's room.

Securing a second rope to a merlon, Dulnear descended into the courtyard, keeping to the darkness. From his new vantage point, he could see that most of the men carried weapons. Quickly assessing the mob, he noticed fighters from at least five different parts of Aun, and some he didn't recognize. They were drinking, telling stories, and some were tossing daggers at something that looked like a straw man secured to a beam. Looking closer, he realized that they were having target practice with the body of Tcharron. His nostrils flared and he suppressed a growl as indignation stirred itself within him.

The man from the north hunched down and crept along the eastern wall, doing his best to stay to the backs of the men in the courtyard. Reaching the door closest to the staircase leading to Ocmallum's chamber, he checked the latch and discovered that it was not locked. *That was too easy*, he thought to himself as he slipped inside.

It was strangely black inside the hall. Dulnear's thoughts raced as he wondered why a corner of the castle that was perpetually occupied would be so dark. He felt around for the stairs leading to his prey and found a heavy, polished handrail that curved upward around a spiral staircase. *It is here*, he thought, and the fine hairs along the back of his neck began to tingle as he ascended upward.

O

"I don't like this," Son exclaimed. He and Faymia had been standing at the base of the castle wall, impatiently waiting for Dulnear's return.

The woman stared up at the battlements, saying nothing. Her jaw was clenched and her hands nervously twitched. Finally speaking up, she said, "I'm going up there. I need to see what's going on," and began to climb the rope.

"I'm going with you," the boy whispered. Tension gripped him, but not knowing what was happening to his friend was a greater dread than risking a closer look. He followed after her and ascended the wall.

The two knelt in the shadows at the top of the battlement. Son tried to discern what was happening below while keeping an eye on the nearest guard. Suddenly, he felt Faymia's hand grip his arm.

"Savages," she whispered, and pointed toward the now mangled body of her former slave boss.

The boy felt a shiver run down his spine as he watched the men toss weapons into Tcharron's corpse. He prayed that he would not become the next target for them to practice with on this night. "Th-That's horrid," he stuttered, and looked away.

"Over there," the woman said, and she gestured toward the northeastern-most door in the courtyard.

Son turned his attention toward the door below. He could see two men walking toward the entrance. They had swords drawn and stepped lightly so as not to be heard as they entered the castle. The boy watched breathlessly as he waited to see what was going to happen. Unexpectedly, the door flew open and the men came tumbling out. Then, the door slammed shut.

"He doesn't know his own strength," Faymia lamented. "We may have to do this the hard way."

The boy exhaled through pursed lips. The woman's words were completely unwelcome. "What do you mean?" he asked.

"Look!" the woman urged.

Son saw that the scuffle, and the unconscious bodies of the two men, had not gone unnoticed and that other mercenaries were now taking an interest in the entrance. The boy's mind raced, and he had to beat fear down as if it were a rabid hound. "What do we do?" he asked.

"You're going to have to go in there after him," she instructed.

"Against all of those men?" the boy protested. "Even with the element of surprise, I'd still end up like Tcharron."

"I'll draw their attention," Faymia explained. "All three of those doors lead to Ocmallum's chamber. Just get inside one of them and cover Dulnear's back."

Before Son had a chance to ask any more questions, the woman withdrew an arrow, fired it at the nearest wall guard, and watched him stumble between two merlons, falling to the ground outside. She then unsheathed her sword and ran toward the guard patrolling the southern wall.

When the boy noticed that the crowd was now moving to check out the melee along the wall, he quickly climbed down into the courtyard and dashed into the nearest door. His heart beat like a hammer and his hands were clammy. Before closing the door behind him, he peeked out to see that Faymia had felled the second guard and was now releasing fire arrows toward the courtyard entrances.

She's as crazy as he is, he thought to himself as he closed the door just before one of her arrows scattered flames against it.

Once inside, Son barred the door and found himself in a dark corridor. Nothing was visible, with the exception of a faint orange light that came down from what appeared to be a staircase in the distance. He could see the silhouette of a man racing up the stairs, and could hear men shouting curses out in the courtyard.

The boy began to run toward the stairs, then stopped himself. Remembering that there were three entrances, he sprinted through the dark hall and barred the other two doors as well. As he did, he tripped over a man that he assumed had been beaten by Dulnear. He stumbled to his feet, began running again, and tripped over another but caught himself before falling to the floor. *I'm glad he's on my side*, he thought, and slowed his pace to keep from tripping on any more.

Reaching the stairs, he withdrew his sword and took a deep breath. Grabbing the railing, he looked up toward the light, hoping to get a better feel for his surroundings. Suddenly, a wounded man came rolling down the stairs, nearly hitting him and taking him down as well.

Son mustered his courage and decided to quicken his pace upward. Before he could get very far, there was the sound of a heavy door slamming shut and all went black.

Dulnear stood in Ocmallum's den. The air held a scent he did not like and did not recognize. In the dimly lit room there was a large, ornate desk surrounded by expensive furnishings to one side, and a bed covered in fine linens on the other. Across from the door, on the opposite side of the round room, was a chair that more resembled a throne than a common armchair. In it sat the slave king himself, with his back toward a massive glass window. He wore a blood-red gown. His beard and hair appeared more disheveled than earlier, and his eyes looked wide and wild. On either side of him stood guards that Dulnear could not place. Their faces were pale and their eyes were vacant, but their bare arms looked as if they were forged in steel.

"So, you're the one causing all the commotion," Ocmallum said with a strange amusement in his voice.

The man from the north had a difficult time reading the room. Normally, he would see only three men and have full confidence that he was in no danger. However, this was different. The slaver held a small lantern in his lap, the only light source in the room. Its flame cast eerie shadows over his face. To make things more difficult, the eyes of his bodyguards betrayed nothing. There wasn't a hint of concern in them. They didn't move and never blinked. Dulnear felt an unnatural fear creep over him. Pushing through his uneasiness, he answered the man, "I am only here for information."

"Oh, I suspect you want more than that," Ocmallum answered with a smile that dripped with guile.

The northerner stood frozen by those words. After standing silent for a moment, he asked, "And what is it you believe I seek?"

"Why, freedom, of course," the man answered with a creepy certainty.

Dulnear suppressed a wry smile as he thought about the old man's words. "I am a free man," he said. "More free than any man on this wretched estate."

"Are you though?" the slaver pressed. Looking Dulnear up and down, he observed, "You're a northerner, and you're here in the south. I'm sure you're trying to distance yourself from your barbaric northern roots, but somehow, you just can't. Is any of this ringing true?"

The man from the north was both stunned and angered by the veracity of Ocmallum's words. All that he had worked to leave behind over the past few seasons seemed to taunt him from underneath the old man's voice. His knees felt weak, and he wanted to strike him down but needed the information he was there to collect. "My burden is my own," he answered as calmly as he could.

"It's not that large a thing," Ocmallum replied. "I could lift it for you, if you'd let me."

"Just information," Dulnear said in a clear, authoritative tone, taking a step forward.

The slave king's face fell. "How incredibly boring you are," he sneered. "I suppose you're looking for someone. Is that why you dragged poor Tcharron here? Now his body rots in my courtyard and it's all your fault."

The man from the north felt queasy upon hearing about Tcharron. Despair, anger, and anxiety beat on his neck, but he continued to stand. Placing his hand on the hilt of his sword, he replied, "I am looking for a young girl."

The old man laughed heartily until he began to cough. "Why didn't you just say so?" he said. "I have many young girls that I would be happy to sell you. I'm sure they would bring you great pleasure."

With each passing moment, Ocmallum appeared older, and somehow more decayed and grotesque to Dulnear. The circles around his eyes became darker and his teeth seemed more jagged. The warrior tightened the grip he had on his sword. Raising his voice, he clarified, "A little girl was taken by one of your crews in Laor. A man called Sevuss was in charge. It was an illegal transfer of life-rights and I have come to bring her home."

"Hmm, little girl, you say. Well then, I suppose I will have to look at my records," the slaver claimed as he stood from his chair, holding the lantern out in front of him. He was somehow taller than he seemed before, and moved in a quick, disorienting fashion.

The man from the north turned his attention toward the desk, expecting to see Ocmallum standing there. Instead, he heard the door slam behind him and the room became black as pitch. Reaching for the latch, he found that the door would not budge. He was trapped.

A searing pain pierced his left side and another his right arm. The strange odor that filled the room seemed to intensify and he had difficulty thinking clearly. Drawing his sword, he swung it wildly in the air but struck nothing. Then, agony began to radiate from his lower back as a dagger was driven into it. Frantically searching his clouded mind, he tried to make sense of what was happening. Pushing aside the now suffocating fear, it dawned on him. *They are blind!*

Dulnear quickly considered his options. If he turned to try to break down the door, he would be dead before he could get it open. His only hope was to take away the silent guards' advantage. Remembering that there was a desk to his right, he ran toward it, twirling his massive sword with his left hand and smashing down hard with his iron-fisted right, eventually knocking over furniture and scattering papers to the floor. Quickly darting behind the desk, he could hear subtle footsteps moving over the papers.

One blind guard was moving toward him from his left, and the other from his right. When he could no longer hear footsteps from his right, he swung his weapon in that direction, catching only the tip of his sword on the man's tunic. At the same time, the sudden whoosh of a blade could be heard beneath his left ear and his shoulder began to bleed.

Furious and disoriented, the man from the north kicked the desk away from him, then spun with his sword, still striking only the air around him. He would continue to fight Ocmallum's guards until he could no longer move.

Until my last breath, Dulnear thought to himself. Then it dawned on him that perhaps the strange odor in the chamber was clouding his mind. He did his best to recall the layout of the room and hoped he was correct about the location of the window. He ran toward it and stumbled into the slaver's throne. Recovering quickly, he tossed the large chair through the window, bringing massive shards of glass crashing to the ground below.

The man from the north breathed in the night air and almost instantly, his mind began to clear. The angst that had been covering his thoughts like a heavy blanket lifted and he was able to gauge the movements of the guards with greater perception. Sensing a blade coming down upon him from behind, he blocked with his sword then spun around, landing a steel-fisted punch on the blind man, sending him reeling back.

The other guard leaped upon Dulnear's back and begun striking him repeatedly. Stabbing pain shot through his shoulder, causing him to drop his sword. He reached behind and grabbed the man's tunic. It seemed that the garment was going to tear, but he managed to peel the guard off of him before it did. He tossed him in the direction of his counterpart. Judging by the commotion, he reckoned that the throw landed true. Unfortunately, he unintentionally kicked his sword along the floor and was now groping desperately for it before the two men launched another attack.

The sound of the guards scrambling to their feet was followed by the clanging of steel. The northern warrior was bleeding freely from his wounds and knew he would not be able to withstand many more. Without his sword, he had little hope.

Unexpectedly, the sound of something striking the ceiling above could be heard, and the room was illuminated by fire. Dulnear could see his sword and he took hold of it. Now that he could see his enemies, he advanced against them.

As one guard leaped at him from his left, he ducked and plunged his sword into the rib cage of the one on his right. The first guard continued his attack, chopping downward toward the back of the northerner's neck. Dulnear spun around quickly and blocked the attack with his metal hand, then kicked the man backward with a powerful boot to the chest.

To the warrior's surprise, the second guard advanced as if there were not blood pouring from his side. The man from the north stepped back, stunned that the man showed no sign of slowing his attack. As the guard slashed inward toward his head, he dodged and brought his sword down upon his shoulder, cleaving off his right arm.

Then the first guard ran back. He swiped toward Dulnear's side, but the warrior trapped the guard's sword with his own. Once disarmed, the blind man growled like an animal and began clawing savagely.

Disgusted and ready to end the battle, the man from the north shoved the guard back with his right fist, then swung his sword around, taking off the man's head. His body fell to its knees, then onto the floor. As it did, Dulnear noticed that the other guard was still crawling along the floor.

The blind, one-armed man felt around on the floor until he came to his own dismembered arm and began to peel the blade out of his own dead hand.

"You must be kidding me!" the man from the north exclaimed. He sheathed his sword, kicked the guard's weapon away and grabbed the man by the leg. As animal barks and hisses poured from the blind man's mouth, Dulnear held him high and flung him out of the large, open window with revulsion.

Taking a deep breath of the night air, he heard a woman's voice yell from below, "You almost hit me with that guy!"

He looked down from the window and saw that Faymia was waiting at the foot of the castle. "Sorry about that!" he yelled back. "And thank you for the light!" he added, pointing toward the fiery arrows lodged in the ceiling.

"You're welcome, my darling," she said. "Now grab Son and get down here. That mob isn't going to stay trapped in the courtyard much longer!"

"Son? Where is he?" he asked.

"He came in after you."

Dulnear's neck tensed as he thought about his friend's safety. He ran toward the door and pounded at it with his metal fist. Realizing that it was taking too long, he ran back toward the desk, pointed it toward the door, and pushed it with all of his might.

The door broke partially off of its hinges, giving the man enough space to get his sword through and remove the bar that was securing it shut from the outside. Breaking through to the vestibule, he could see Son standing over the slave king with a sword to his neck.

"A secret path on the north side of the road," the boy exclaimed. "Just east of Redbramble!"

The man on the floor quivered and pleaded for his life. Dulnear fought back the urge to run him through and send him flying out the window to join his bodyguard. "Down the stairs and through the front gate," he instructed his young friend with a forced calmness.

Son nodded and quickly headed down the stairs. As the man from the north followed, he grabbed the lantern that Ocmallum took with him when he locked the warrior in his chamber. As he stepped over the slaver, he could hear the man gasp in panic. Turning to address him, he snarled, "You are a pathetic man. Pray that you never see me again, or I'll burn more than the ceiling of your bedchamber."

Dulnear wasn't certain, but he thought he saw an odd smile creep over the old man's face. He then spun around and darted down the staircase to catch up with Son.

Reaching the bottom of the stairs, Son could hear the clamor of the mob out in the courtyard. It was dark, but he remembered that the castle was longer than it was wide. If he moved away from the courtyard doors, he should find a way out and reach the portcullis quickly.

All of a sudden, there was a sound of shattering wood and the voices of the men outside became louder. They had broken through the door at the opposite end of the hall and were pouring inside. The boy had just begun to dart away from the commotion when a large, metallic hand tapped him on the shoulder.

He startled and looked behind him to see his friend Dulnear standing there with a lantern in his hand. "Hold this," the man said, handing off the light. He then withdrew his sword and added, "Quickly, lead us out of here. I will guard our backs."

Son sprinted through the halls of the manor, surprised that it was so dark and empty. There seemed to be no occupants other than Ocmallum and his soldiers. He would have dwelled on the observation longer had the slaver's crew not been growing louder.

"That way," the man from the north directed.

The boy could see a large wooden door that was barred shut from the inside. His friend moved forward to remove the bolt, and he could smell the night air rush into the castle. Just outside the door was the portcullis, lowered shut.

"Let us go!" Dulnear urged, running toward the gate.

"What about the gate guard?" the boy asked.

"Already taken care of," the northerner stated as he gestured toward the arrow-ridden body hanging from the wall.

As they reached the gate, Son looked around for a winch to raise the bars. "Where are the ropes?" he asked, feeling fear and desperation build in his chest.

"No time for that!" Dulnear stated urgently. He then sheathed his sword, reached down, and threw the portcullis above his head. "Go!" he shouted.

Son ran past his friend and turned around, spying lights moving inside. "I see torches!" he exclaimed.

The man from the north glanced over his shoulder, took a deep breath, and ran forward, allowing the barred entrance to fall behind him. "Quickly!" he shouted.

The night was black, and the boy could see very little. He reached out and grabbed his friend's long fur coat, afraid that they might become separated. His steps were much shorter than his long-legged companion, and he struggled to keep up. Unexpectedly, a cold voice could be heard from the high corner of the castle, stopping them both in their tracks.

"You should have killed me, boy!" the voice of the slaver king rang out in the darkness.

"Did you hear that?" Son asked his friend.

"Pay no attention," the northerner replied. "He is only trying to sow fear. Intimidation is his greatest weapon."

Son swallowed and tried to push the mounting angst away. He was about to move forward when the voice called out again.

"You should have run me through when you had the chance! Now she will have to die."

The boy shook, and a tear formed in his eye. "What are we going to do?" he asked.

"Keep moving forward," the warrior said. "Do not let his words dampen your courage."

Son wiped the tear from his eye and set his mind to rescuing Maren. But what little fortitude he had seemed to melt away as Ocmallum's voice seemed to grow louder and more ominous.

"Gale Hill Farm!" the old man yelled.

The boy's knees threatened to buckle. He felt exposed and defeated. "Dulnear!" was all he could think to say.

The man from the north said nothing, but the boy could feel him breathing more heavily.

Suddenly, the noise behind them grew louder and he reckoned that the soldiers had reached the portcullis. "They're gaining," he warned, with more than a hint of desperation.

"There!" Dulnear whispered back, beginning to plow forward.

In the distance, the boy could see a torch glowing. His instinct screamed to reach it as fast as he could. He let go of the northerner's coat and ran as though his life depended on it. Like a drowning man racing for the surface of the water, he shot through the darkness until he was upon Faymia and the horses, with his friend close behind him.

Gesturing with the torch, the woman urged from atop her steed, "Quickly, mount up! We must ride hard and ride fast."

Son hopped onto the horse's back behind her, and Dulnear mounted the other animal.

"Toward Redbramble," the man from the north instructed. "If we ride through the night, we should be there by first light."

"But it's dark as soot," the boy answered.

"Then we take our chances," the man said, moving out onto the path that led back toward Dorcadas. "If Ocmallum dispatches soldiers to fortify the slaver camp, and they reach it before we do, then all of this will have been for naught."

Son looked out into the void of night. He knew it would be dangerous, but the men approaching from the castle would be even more so. He swallowed and responded, "Then let's go."

CHAPTER FIFTEEN
A Heart to Fight For

AS MAREN STOOD IN HER cage, she wondered what was to become of her. Her pen was the only one that was locked, and as she watched the other slaves come and go, she felt a strange emotion that was one part jealousy and one part sadness for those souls (herself included) that had exchanged their freedom and dignity for sweets and amusements.

Noticing a plump woman walk by with a piece of blackberry pie, her stomach turned. *I never want another slice of that as long as I live*, she thought to herself. She sat down and leaned back against the bars. As she reclined there, she remembered the words that the old man said to her in Ahmcathare.

"I'm a part of the Great Father's story," she said to herself with a sigh. She then wrapped her arms around her knees and closed her eyes.

"Hey," she thought she heard someone say, breaking her rumination.

"Little girl," the voice said again.

Maren opened her eyes and looked around. In the cage next to hers was a young man with unruly, brown hair. He wore a deep-blue tunic that he kept neatly buttoned up despite its unclean condition. Sitting there, he leaned against the bars of his enclosure and peered at her.

"What is it?" she asked.

"Why can't you leave your cage?" the man inquired.

"I ran away," she answered plainly.

"Why would you do that?" he asked.

Maren thought for a moment. She didn't enjoy working for Kugun at all, and she hated the idea of going to a brothel. Turning so she could see the man's eyes, she said, "Because I was made to be free," she stated. "And so were you."

The man stared curiously at her for a moment, then replied, "Well, it looks like we may have missed the mark on that." His eyes fell and his lips continued to move. However, Maren couldn't hear a thing the man was saying.

The girl paused for a moment as she held her gaze on him. "You were made to be powerful, and heroic," she added. "Not a slave to plays and pies." She then leaned back again and stared out into the night as the commotion in the camp died down and people began to settle in. As she watched, her eyes grew heavy and her mind contemplated what it meant to endure the pain of living in the real world.

"Pssst," the young man whispered, interrupting her thoughts.

"Yes?"

"Thank you."

Maren remembered how she had squeezed through the bars of her cage in Ahmcathare. It was difficult, but not impossible. She looked around and knew that she could do the same thing here if not for the guards that regularly passed by. It frustrated her, but she still held onto a fragment of hope. "You're welcome," she finally replied to the man, and went back to her contemplations until she slipped into a deep sleep.

○

It was nearly pitch-dark in the town square of Redbramble. Son, Dulnear, and Faymia had ridden all the way from Dorcadas without stopping, and the horses needed a brief respite. There was a trough outside of the village pub and the animals drank heartily as the three travelers stood together and discussed their plan to liberate Maren.

"Do you think they're following us?" Son whispered. With the exception of a small number of people inside the tavern, the entire town had turned in for the night, and he didn't want to rouse anyone.

"I do not know," the man from the north answered in a hushed tone.

"What if they are?" the boy asked. He was exhausted, anxious, and shaken from the events of the day. The fear of being captured by Ocmallum's mercenaries was nearly suffocating. "I don't want to end up like Tcharron," he added.

"We are few, and traveling light," Faymia tried to assure him. "If they did decide to pursue us, it's likely that they're still trying to organize themselves."

"There is a chance that the slaver would not waste his resources," Dulnear added. "He deals in fear and intimidation masterfully. When I faced his guards, he went as far as to employ a strange incense that caused a terrible sense of dread to come over me. I have never experienced anything like it."

Faymia leaned in to examine her husband. The dried

blood on his neck and coat appeared as black stains in the dim light. "I despise them," she declared. "They lure people in with delights they don't need, have them believing that they can't live without them, then oppress them to keep their loyalty."

"I agree," the man from the north concurred. "However, our sole focus should be on retrieving Maren. When she is returned to us, then we shall worry about pursuers and slaver injustices."

Son breathed deeply of the damp midnight air. He fought off thoughts of Gale Hill Farm ruined, slaver ambushes, and violence. He imagined finally arriving back at his home just to collect his things and leave. The peace he felt from sharing life with his companions there was evaporating and insecurity was nagging at his heart. "Well then," he said. "We shouldn't stay here any longer. Let's go get her."

○

"Go free!" Maren shouted with a voice that echoed liked thunder through the forest.

In her dream, she was out of her cage and there was fire all around. Though the flames were approaching the circle of pens, the people inside of them sat passively and refused to get out.

"What's wrong with you?!" she pleaded. "Death is upon you, and all you can do is sit there!"

As she stood in the center of the camp, she gazed into the faces of the slaves. Some she knew from Laor, yet others were unfamiliar and difficult to make out. Though there was not a single pen locked, they insisted upon remaining caged like animals.

"You were made for more!" she continued. "Have you forgotten who you are? You are mothers and fathers! You are daughters and sons!"

As she continued to cry out, the stubbornness on the faces of some of the slaves began to melt, and Maren could see tears forming in their eyes.

"You were meant to hold your heads high! You were meant to carry dignity and reflect glory!" she boomed, with tears now flowing down her own face. "Why would you give that away for pie and shows?!"

Now, the flames were burning higher, and the slavers appeared around her. Their appearance was larger, more menacing, and distorted somehow. They startled her for a moment but, when she noticed some of the slaves pushing against the doors of their pens, she was filled with a fresh boldness.

"Remember who you are!" she urged, and some of them started out into the circle to join her. "Remember what you once dreamed!"

Soon, the mangled-looking slavers were surrounding her more closely. They were contorted and angry, and they were ready to pour their wrath upon her for encouraging their source of gold to go free. "You will die for this!" one of the monstrous-looking men raged before reaching out for the girl with his gangly arms.

Maren ducked and rolled out of harm's way, then ran past each cage shouting, "Be free! Remember! Live fully!" As she did, she could see that some of the slaves were now weeping in remorse. They sobbed and covered their faces in shame, but remained prisoners.

"We deserve to burn!" one woman yelled as the girl ran by.

"No!" Maren cried as her face burned red with sweat and tears, and she pleaded all the louder.

A hideous cackle filled the air as the gnarled slavers laughed gloatingly at the penitent woman's statement. "That's right! No one would want you now, anyway!"

The young girl's desperation turned to indignation upon hearing the laughter of the slavers. Running to the woman, she called through the bars, "That's what they want you to believe! The door is unlocked. You can have your beauty back! Come out!"

A warm, clammy hand wrapped around Maren's shoulder and spun her around. The slavers were now too closely upon her for her to run away. "You will all burn," they said in unison through twisted, blackened mouths.

Fear gripped the girl and she felt unable to breathe. Mustering all of her strength, she was only able to force out a quiet whisper to the slaves, "You were made for more."

Raising her hands in defense, she expected to receive a fatal blow from the evil gang surrounding her, but it didn't come. Instead, all went black and gray, and she could hear mighty shouts coming from the slaves that had come out of their cages.

○

The night's darkness still fought against the light of the morning but, through the early dawn haze, Maren could see panicked legs dashing to and fro around her cage. The clanging of steel and the pained cries of injured men snapped her out of her slumber and she sat up, squinting through the mist to see what was happening.

Breaking through the gray-black sky were fiery arrows being launched from just outside the camp. As they struck tents and caravans, men screamed and ran. It was a hurricane of terror and commotion. The fact that the girl's cage was locked heightened her sense of helplessness. She was trapped inside the maelstrom and couldn't get out. She was still afraid that she would be caught trying to squeeze through the bars.

Maren could see a figure moving through the madness. It was all rage, and steel—and fur. Immediately, she knew, and shouted, "Dulnear!"

The man from the north continued through the camp like a man on fire, cutting down slavers like wheat in season. As the girl violently shook the door of her pen, a young voice broke through, "Stay in your cages! You will be free soon but stay in your cages!"

"Son!" she called out.

"Maren!" his voice rang through the thick, smoky morning air.

"I'm over here!" she cried.

The boy ran to the cage and reached through the bars to touch her. "We found you!" he crowed.

Upon seeing the face of her guardian, the girl was awash with a sense of comfort. Many words flowed through her mind, but what came out of her mouth was, "I'm sorry."

Son's eyebrows shot up and he looked surprised by her apology. "There'll be plenty of time for that later," he said. "For now, we need to get you out of here," and he smashed the lock with the hilt of his sword.

"Can I come with you?" a voice asked. It was the young man in the blue tunic beginning to exit his pen.

"No!" Son yelled. "That northerner will cut down anyone he doesn't recognize and is not in a cage. If you value your life, then stay put until he says that it's safe to come out."

As Maren stepped out to join Son, she hugged his waist tightly, almost pushing him off of his feet. "Thank you!" she burst.

The boy took her by the hand and began to lead her toward the path that headed out to the road. "You can thank me when we get home," he said, and walked quickly with his sword at the ready.

Before they were able to go very far, the man with the long, gray hair stepped out in front of them. "Where do you think you're going, Maren?" he asked. His usual amiable demeanor was gone and he clutched a hammer in his hand.

"I'm going home!" the girl declared, and she began to step forward.

Holding his ground, the man objected, "You belong to Sevuss. You will be going nowhere! Get back in your cage before I break your arms!"

Son drew his arm back to strike the man but, before he could extend his blade, a blur of coat and steel swept in front of him, carrying the man away. Turning his surprised eyes toward the girl, he insisted, "Let's go!"

Maren could hear the dirty-haired man pleading for his life in the distance. She had never seen Dulnear like this before and was both frightened and relieved at the same time. From out of the smoke and confusion, she heard the northerner's voice yell out, "Maren, take this!" and a blade was flung through the air, landing at her feet.

"It's a sword!" the girl exclaimed.

"Grab it!" Son instructed. "You may need it before we reach the horses."

"Indeed," she smiled widely, and snatched the weapon from the ground.

Son could see the path leading out of the camp and darted toward it. There was so much confusion between the burning caravans and Dulnear violently whirling about that no one seemed to be paying any attention to him.

Pulling Maren along, they were just beyond the circle of cages when he felt an intense pain in the back of his left leg. Spinning around to see what happened, he noticed a ginger-haired, leathery-skinned man and a young boy running toward them.

"That's Micah!" Maren announced.

Son reached back to discover that a knife was partially embedded in his leg. Clenching his jaw, he pulled it out and forced it into the ground. "And who's that man with him?" he asked through gritted teeth.

Before the girl had a chance to answer, Sevuss and his son were upon them. "Where are you going with my slave?" the man demanded.

"My friends came to take me home!" Maren shouted.

"So YOU brought this upon us!" the slaver reckoned. "That northerner has killed half my crew, my tents are destroyed, and my slaves are running off!"

"I am her guardian," Son spoke up. "I, and the man from the north. We did not sign for her life-rights to be taken, so you have her illegally!"

Sevuss's face turned red and his fists curled tightly. "Do you hear that, boy?" he asked Micah with a sarcastic grin. "What do I always tell you?"

"That the law only applies to those who can't buy their way out of it," the boy answered with a proud smirk.

"There's not much we couldn't get away with doing to the two of you," the slaver boasted as he reached down to pull his knife out of the ground. "I could gut you like a fish and the authorities would just look the other way."

Son suddenly noticed that his leg was throbbing with pain, and he tried to keep his weight off of it. Bolstering his confidence, he replied, "You won't be getting away with anything, stinkmonger! Maren and I are leaving here and there's nothing you can do about it!"

"What?" the slaver croaked. "Did you just call me a stinkmonger?"

"Of course I did," the boy continued, hoping that his aggression would overtake the pain in his leg. "You smell like a vomiting armpit!"

Micah glared at Son, then turned his gaze to his father. "Are you going to let him speak to you like that?" he asked.

"Quiet!" Sevuss snapped, clearly riled by Son's insults. "I'll tell you what, ragamuffin; if Maren wants to fight my son for her freedom, I will give it to her."

Son was taken aback by the man's offer. He was certain that, no matter what happened, the slaver would not be agreeing to let Maren go today. Hoping that Dulnear would be along to assist them soon, he agreed. "Okay, but you have to promise not to cry when your little lad is beaten by an even littler girl."

Sevuss snarled behind tobacco-stained teeth, then

looked at his son. Handing his knife to him, he instructed, "Don't end it too quickly. I want to enjoy the show."

Micah confidently held the blade out in front of him and made a slicing motion through the air. "As you wish," he hissed.

"I don't agree to that," Son protested.

Maren stepped forward with her sword firmly in hand. "It's okay," she said. She glanced briefly back at Son, who also had a solid grip on the hilt of his weapon. "Part of a bigger story," she whispered to herself.

As Son watched, every muscle in his body tensed and he thought about every action he could possibly take if he felt the fight was going unfavorably. He wanted desperately to just stop it now and take his chances with fleeing on a wounded leg.

The two children stood face-to-face. The young boy looked down on Maren, murmuring insults with a stony expression. As he raised the knife over his head to strike, there was a high-pitched whoosh, and his left ear fell to the ground.

"Ear!" the girl yelled, pulling her sword back to the ready position.

The boy looked down to see his bloody ear laying in the grass and stumbled backward with disbelief. "You...you cut off my—"

"Ear!" Maren yelled again, this time catching only the lobe of the right ear.

"Micah!" Sevuss called out as he ran to the boy, catching him in his arms. Wiping the blood from his son's face, the slave master growled at the girl, "You cut up my beautiful boy!"

"Now I can go free," Maren reminded the man sternly.

Sevuss gently laid his son down in the grass, then stood to face the girl. "I'll set you free, Maren. Free to feel pain, free to bleed, and free to die!" He then took the knife from Micah's hand and began to charge her.

Before he could reach the girl, Son stepped in and swept his sword low, hacking the man's shin and causing him to tumble to the ground. "Leave her be!" he yelled. "Or I'll take your ears too!"

Sevuss grabbed his leg and groaned in pain. "I'll kill you, boy!" he proclaimed. He then hoisted himself to his feet and ran at Son as he released a slew of curses.

Son tried to step out of the man's way, but his own wounded leg held him back. Sevuss tackled him, kneeled on his arms, and raised his knife to plunge it into the boy's neck. "No!" the boy yelled, and he pulled his left arm loose just in time to hold the blade back. As he did, he could see Maren come up behind the slaver and pound him repeatedly with the pommel of her sword.

The man howled like an alarmed fox and swiped backward with his knife.

Seizing the distraction, Son wrenched his right arm free. They were too close for him to use his sword, so he made a stone-like fist and punched the man in the mouth, sending a brown tooth sailing through the air.

Sevuss coughed, then wiped his mouth. Without saying a word, he raised his knife once more. Suddenly, he dropped it and the ends of two of his fingers fell to the ground.

"Fingers!" Maren yelled as she stood over the man.

Like an animal, the slaver roared, spun around, and sprang at Maren. But before he could fully get to his feet,

Son was on his shoulders, pounding furiously on his already wounded head.

Ignoring the pain and bleeding from his leg, the boy continued to punch and thrash, and would not relent. Finally, the man fell face-first to the ground, letting out a warbled groan of agony as he slipped into unconsciousness.

○

Maren stood over Sevuss with weapon in hand and arms shaking. Everything in her wanted to plunge her sword into the man's body, but she knew that it was not right to kill for spite. Turning around, she saw Micah, now sitting up, holding his ear in his hand. There were tears of hatred in his eyes as he glared at her.

Maren walked over to the boy. "I thought you were my friend," she said with eyebrows pressed low.

"I was never your friend," the boy answered. "My father said you were a mark, so I did what he said." He then added, "Besides, who would ever want to be friends with a gray-mind imbecile like you?"

The words cut deep into Maren's heart, though she did not show it. She had yearned for friendship her whole life but found it in very short supply. The disappointment she felt by Micah's betrayal was like an anchor around her neck. She searched her mind for the words to say, and finally replied, "I am not less."

"What?! What's that supposed to mean?" the boy snipped. "It's like you're not all there!"

Maren looked down at the boy's ear, then back up to his bleeding face. "Then we are the same," she said.

"I hate you!" Micah cried out. "I'll get you for what you've done!"

Just then, Son appeared next to her. Placing his hand on the girl's shoulder, he spoke to the boy. "I'm sorry it had to be this way," he said. Then his expression changed, and he did something Maren was not expecting. He stepped closer to the boy, lowered himself onto one knee, and offered, "Why don't you come with us?"

"Come with you?!" the boy shrilled. He glanced at his unconscious father, then back at Son. "Just stay away from me, and take your broken ward with you!"

Suddenly, Maren noticed the young man with the dark-blue tunic jog by, as did several of the other slaves from the camp. Then Dulnear appeared, looking rather pale and exhausted. "It is time to go," the northerner said. "Make your way to Faymia."

It was lighter now, and the girl surveyed the camp where she had been enslaved. The caravans burned, and bodies littered the ground like rubbish after a festival. She turned her eyes toward Dulnear, whose blood ran from under his coat. "Are you okay?" she asked the man.

He met the girl's eyes briefly and smiled weakly, then answered, "I am now that I am with you again."

She then reached up and took his arm, walking with him behind Son. Soon they were with Faymia and the horses, who were now waiting for them on the path, midway to the road. When she saw the woman, she ran to her and threw her arms around her waist.

Faymia picked her up and held her tightly, beginning to weep. Maren placed her head on the woman's shoulder and gently stroked her hair. "Thank you for coming for me," she said.

"We are not home yet," the man from the north reminded them as he mounted his horse. "Son, would you mind taking the reins?" he added.

The boy hopped on in front of Dulnear while Faymia and Maren rode together. Once they were on the road toward Laor, Maren felt a sense of peace, and looked forward to seeing the farm again.

CHAPTER SIXTEEN
Return to Laor

MAREN RODE ALONG, SITTING IN front of Son. There had to be some rearranging of horses earlier since the girl felt the other one emitted an odor that no one else detected. Occasionally, the boy would let her take the horse's reins and direct the animal. They were surrounded by the other recently released slaves. They were chatting on about life-rights, legalities, and the like. Faymia walked nearby, leading Dulnear's horse as he slept. They had been on the road together for some time and were approaching Laor.

"Son?" the girl spoke up.

"Yes?"

"Can I say that I'm sorry now?" she asked.

The boy took a deep breath and replied, "I suppose so."

"I'm sorry that I caused so much trouble," she said with her eyes still on the road ahead.

Son waited a moment to speak. Maren could tell by his breathing that he was carefully considering what to say. "You know, I would run the length of Aun, and back again, to make sure you were okay," he began. "You're my sister and I love you dearly." He then paused again before continuing. "But even more difficult than breaking through a castle's defenses, fighting slavers, and riding through the night, is the pain I feel from your dishonesty with me."

The girl glanced over at the wounded man from the north, then at his wife, who was wiping tears from her eyes as she led his horse. Something stirred inside of her that couldn't fully be called remorse, but couldn't be called indifference either. Her chest felt heavy, and she knew she didn't want her friends to suffer on her behalf again. "I'm very sorry," she said. "I wish that I would have listened."

"Me too," the boy said. "I was afraid we wouldn't be able to find you. We had to go to the king of slavers himself to find out where you were."

Maren shuddered at the thought of a slaver king. Just being with a slave *owner* was bad enough. "I was in Ahmcathare for a little while," she stated.

"Ahmcathare?" the boy sputtered. "What were you doing there?"

"I worked for a fat tool seller," she said plainly.

"Oh," the boy said. "How did you end up back at the camp?"

"I walked," she explained. "Well, most of the way. A funny man named Treyvin gave me a ride too."

"What happened to the tool seller?" he asked.

"He was going to take me to a brothel, so I ran away."

"Ran away? How did you manage that?"

"An old man told me the same thing you did, so I slipped out of my cage and ran."

"An old man?" Son asked.

Maren could hear that her guardian was now breathing more deeply, but couldn't tell why. "He was in my cage with me and told me that I was made for more."

"What did he look like?" the boy asked.

"He had white hair and was tall and strong. He was cooking food. He was there one moment, then gone."

Son sniffed, and his shoulders shook. He was quiet for quite some time as they continued along. Finally, he said, "I've seen him too. And every day since, I've thought about it."

Maren looked over at Dulnear's sleeping form draped across the back of his horse. She admired his courage and strength and wished to be more like him. "Is he going to be okay?" she asked.

Son wiped a tear from his eye and observed the man from the north. "He'll recover," he answered. "He always does."

The townspeople of Laor gathered around, welcoming back their family members who had gone off with Sevuss and his crew. There were many tears and even more questions. Maren watched as they embraced each other and shared stories of the past few weeks. She also noticed that several of the shops had been boarded up, and the once tidy village appeared rather unkempt.

"Will it go back?" she asked Son.

"I sure hope so," the boy answered. "I have never known a place like Laor. I wish the slavers would just walk off the end of Aun and never come back."

"I agree," the tired, deep voice of Dulnear said from

behind them. He was sitting on his horse now, and the blood on his hand and face was dried and black.

"That giant bloke over there mowed them down like grass!" someone shouted. "I never seen anything like it!"

"'Twas nothing," the aching man from the north said.

It tickled Maren that her friend was receiving so much attention, so she moved closer to his horse and put her hand on his leg.

"You have fans," Faymia pointed out, still standing there with the reins.

The warrior chuckled quietly and admitted, "I suppose I do. However, I think we should make our way home. I have many wounds that need tending, and my bed is calling."

"As you wish, giant bloke," his wife said with a smile, and she joined him atop the horse.

Son and Maren mounted their horse as well and, as they rode out of the village, the girl looked back and hoped it would again be what it once was.

They traveled in silence, tired and sore. Eventually, home could be seen from their stretch of the road.

As they approached Gale Hill Farm, a strange sensation that the world was different arose in Maren. She noticed that much was overgrown and the house looked derelict, but the garden seemed to have been ravaged by animals. Though it still carried a sense of home, it was shabbier than she remembered it. As they approached the house, the front door appeared to have been kicked in.

"Wait!" the man from the north cautioned. "It may not be safe."

"I'll go inside and look," Son volunteered, dismounting the horse and withdrawing his sword.

Faymia held out her bow and placed an arrow in it. "I'll cover you from here," she said. "If there's anyone in there, run out the door as fast as you can and I'll make sure they never pay us a visit again."

The boy tightened his grip on the sword and stepped into the doorway. As Maren watched, her heart beat rapidly and she began to massage her ear. "Be careful," she whispered.

After being inside for a few moments, Son called out, "Hey!"

Suddenly there was a horrific yell, followed by a crash as the boy came bursting through the window. Dulnear got down off his horse and withdrew his sword. Standing over his friend, he asked, "What did you see?"

Son struggled to breathe, and he painfully coughed out, "M-m-m-muuule."

"Earl!" Maren shouted. She jumped down from her horse so quickly that she landed on her bottom. Springing up, she ran into the house and immediately came back out leading her donkey by a rope.

Dulnear assisted the boy to his feet and Faymia joined them at the doorway. The four of them looked at each other with a knowing stare, then tiredly began to clean the mess that Earl had left in the house.

CHAPTER SEVENTEEN

The Wisdom of Mules

MAREN WORKED IN THE GARDEN under the early afternoon light. As she did, she whistled the tune she'd learned from Athas. Though they had been home for several days, there was still much to be done to bring the farm back to a presentable state. There were plenty of vines and roots left behind after Earl devoured the garden in their absence, and the ground needed to be prepared for a new planting season.

Appearing at the edge of the field, Son complimented, "This is looking really nice, Maren."

Somewhat shaken from her thoughts and the tune in her head, the girl peered back at the boy and said, "Thank you. I should be done soon." She still wore the apron that Athas had given her, and it was so covered in soil that the embroidered flowers were no longer visible.

"It's okay," Son said. "I was hoping you would take a break so I could show you something."

Maren was curious about the boy's request, since he had

never asked her to take a break before. "Um, okay," she said. "I've been working this whole time."

"I know," he assured her. "Just come with me for a little bit."

"Okay," she answered. She placed her dirty hand on her ear and began to massage it as she made her way to her friend.

Son took her free hand and led her toward the southern edge of Gale Hill Farm. As they neared their destination, Dulnear and Faymia could be seen waiting for them. "What is it?" the girl asked.

"You'll see. It's special," her friend answered.

"Special!" she chirped, and she let go of the boy's hand and ran out to her friends. When she reached them, she noticed that they were standing in a giant ring of climbing violet, filled with dried flower petals. In the center of the ring were three vases cast in iron. She recognized the first vase as the one Dulnear made for Son to honor his mother. "What are the other two?" she asked as she approached.

Faymia walked out and took the girl's hand. Leading her into the circle, she explained, "We wanted to do something for your mum and dad."

Son stood behind the girl and placed his hands on her shoulders. "It didn't seem right that we never remembered them properly," he said. "They were just left under that stone on the road to Blackcloth."

The feelings of that day began to escape from whatever box they had been stuffed into, and sorrow washed over Maren like warm water. She turned and wrapped her arms around Son and wept deeply.

Dulnear knelt behind her, placing his hand on her back.

"I am so sorry, and I am so honored that you came to be a part of our family," he consoled through tears.

Faymia joined him and added, "You have my heart like no one else."

When Maren had found her composure, she knelt in front of the vases that Dulnear had crafted. "Brae" she said, reading the memorial to Son's mother. "Darra," she continued, reading her father's name. Then, her shoulders began to shake and her eyes turned red and full as she read, "Eifa. Mother. I miss you so."

Her friends knelt beside her and wept along with her. As they did, they asked all about the girl's parents and learned more about them in that short time than they did the entire time they had known her. When she had told all of the stories she had wanted to tell, she scooped up handfuls of flower petals and placed them inside the vases. She then encouraged her friends to do the same before they stood.

"Thank you," she said to her friends.

As Son and Maren walked back to the garden together, the girl scratched her head and murmured, "I thought it was supposed to be special."

"What's that?" the boy asked.

"I thought it was going to be something special."

"Wasn't it?"

"No, it was sad. It wasn't special."

"I'm sorry," the boy apologized.

"Thank you, though," Maren said, and she skipped off to the garden to finish her chores.

Maren stood on a rock, eye to eye with Earl. It was mid-morning, and birds were floating across the gray sky as their early songs turned into midday chatter. The freshly broken ground of the garden carried a rich scent that was carried along by a gentle breeze.

"Well, Smarmy Kidd Black," she said, gazing sternly at the mule. "I suppose you think you're going to get away with it, don't you."

Earl gently nudged the girl's shoulder, then lowered his head to take a bite of the lush, cool grass at his feet. Bringing his eyes back up to meet hers, he exhaled sharply through his nostrils and shook his head.

"You can't run forever," Maren added, this time with slightly less authority. She then pushed her mouth to the side and looked around the garden. She could hear Dulnear and Faymia finishing the repairs around the house. They were required after Earl's occupation during their absence. She could also hear Son in the shed making new toys to sell in town.

The donkey brayed, pulling her attention back onto himself.

Startled at first, the girl giggled to herself in amusement. "So that's it, eh, Kidd Black?" she asked. She waited for a reply, but none came. There were only the birds singing, the breeze blowing, and her family working to make their house a home. Once again, she whistled the tune she had learned from Athas. It made her feel light and peaceful. Getting down off the rock, she scratched the mule behind his ears. "Thanks for playing with me, Earl," she said. "I'm going in the barn to help Son."

Whistling her way to the barn, Maren noticed the

accompaniment that the wind through the tall grass provided. The scented air and whispering breeze seemed to make the tune come alive. Opening the door, her heart beat just a little faster. She had chosen her world, and somehow knew that her story would be greater than anything she had ever read.

I hope you enjoyed reading *Daughter of Two Worlds*. Its characters and their adventures are near and dear to me. If you would like information about the next book in the Aun series, as well as other forthcoming projects, please visit my website at www.leebezotte.com and sign up for my e-newsletter. You can also join me on Facebook and Twitter.

Thank you for journeying with me!

Lee Bezotte